OVERDUE JUSTICE

JUSTICE #19

M A COMLEY

New York Times and USA Today bestselling author M A Comley
Published by Jeamel Publishing limited
Copyright © 2019 M A Comley
Digital Edition, License Notes

All rights reserved. This book or any portion thereof may not be reproduced, stored in a retrieval system, transmitted in any form or by any means electronic or mechanical, including photocopying, or used in any manner whatsoever without the express written permission of the author, except for the use of brief quotations in a book review or scholarly journal.

This is a work of fiction. Names, characters, places and incidents are a product of the author's imagination or are used fictitiously, and any resemblance to actual persons living or dead, business establishments, events or locales is entirely coincidental.

OTHER BOOKS BY M A COMLEY

Blind Justice (Novella)

Cruel Justice (Book #1)

Mortal Justice (Novella)

Impeding Justice (Book #2)

Final Justice (Book #3)

Foul Justice (Book #4)

Guaranteed Justice (Book #5)

Ultimate Justice (Book #6)

Virtual Justice (Book #7)

Hostile Justice (Book #8)

Tortured Justice (Book #9)

Rough Justice (Book #10)

Dubious Justice (Book #11)

Calculated Justice (Book #12)

Twisted Justice (Book #13)

Justice at Christmas (Short Story)

Prime Justice (Book #14)

Heroic Justice (Book #15)

Shameful Justice (Book #16)

Immoral Justice (Book #17)

Toxic Justice (Book #18)

Overdue Justice (Book #19)

Unfair Justice (a 10,000 word short story)

Irrational Justice (a 10,000 word short story)

Seeking Justice (a 15,000 word novella)

Caring For Justice (a 24,000 word novella coming July 2019)

Clever Deception (co-written by Linda S Prather)
Tragic Deception (co-written by Linda S Prather)
Sinful Deception (co-written by Linda S Prather)
Forever Watching You (DI Miranda Carr thriller)
Wrong Place (DI Sally Parker thriller #1)
No Hiding Place (DI Sally Parker thriller #2)
Cold Case (DI Sally Parker thriller #3)
Deadly Encounter (DI Sally Parker thriller #4)
Lost Innocence (DI Sally Parker thriller #5)
Web of Deceit (DI Sally Parker Novella with Tara Lyons)
The Missing Children (DI Kayli Bright #1)
Killer On The Run (DI Kayli Bright #2)
Hidden Agenda (DI Kayli Bright #3)
Murderous Betrayal (Kayli Bright #4)
Dying Breath (Kayli Bright #5)
The Hostage Takers (DI Kayli Bright Novella)
No Right to Kill (DI Sara Ramsey #1)
Killer Blow (DI Sara Ramsey #2)
The Dead Can't Speak (DI Sara Ramsey #3)
Deluded (DI Sara Ramsey #4)
The Murder Pact (DI Sara Ramsey #5) Coming August 2019
The Caller (co-written with Tara Lyons)
Evil In Disguise – a novel based on True events
Deadly Act (Hero series novella)
Torn Apart (Hero series #1)
End Result (Hero series #2)
In Plain Sight (Hero Series #3)
Double Jeopardy (Hero Series #4)
Sole Intention (Intention series #1)

Grave Intention (Intention series #2)

Devious Intention (Intention #3)

Merry Widow (A Lorne Simpkins short story)

It's A Dog's Life (A Lorne Simpkins short story)

A Time To Heal (A Sweet Romance)

A Time For Change (A Sweet Romance)

High Spirits

The Temptation series (Romantic Suspense/New Adult Novellas)

Past Temptation

Lost Temptation

KEEP IN TOUCH WITH THE AUTHOR:

Twitter
https://twitter.com/Melcom1

Blog
http://melcomley.blogspot.com

Facebook
http://smarturl.it/sps7jh

Newsletter
http://smarturl.it/8jtcvv

BookBub
www.bookbub.com/authors/m-a-comley

ACKNOWLEDGMENTS

Thank you as always to my rock, Jean, I'd be lost without you in my life.

Special thanks as always go to @studioenp for their superb cover design expertise.

My heartfelt thanks go to my wonderful editor Emmy Ellis, my proofreaders Joseph, Barbara and Jacqueline for spotting all the lingering nits.

A special shoutout to all the wonderful Bloggers and Facebook groups for their never-ending support of my work.

Thank you to Claire Frost for allowing me to use her name as a character in this book.

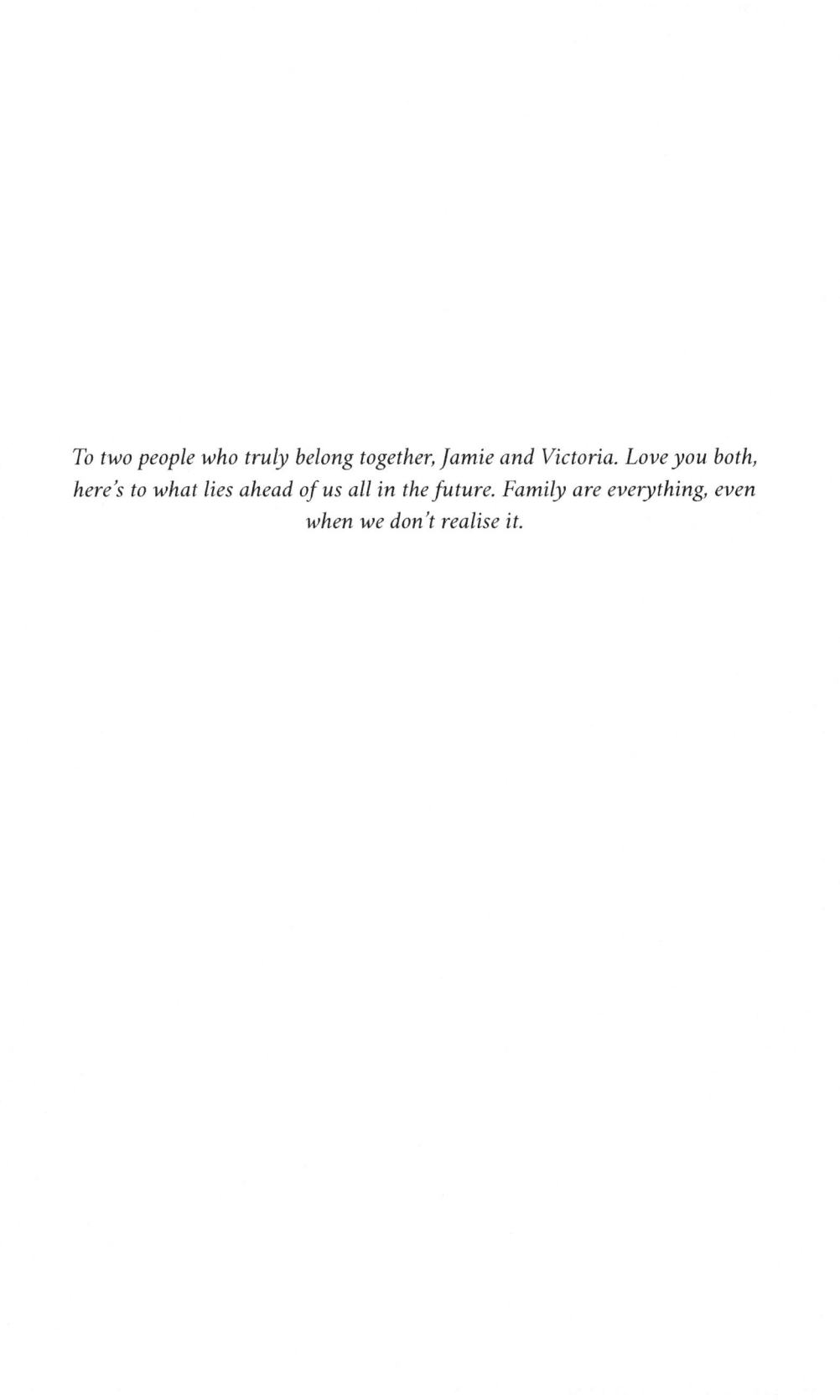

To two people who truly belong together, Jamie and Victoria. Love you both, here's to what lies ahead of us all in the future. Family are everything, even when we don't realise it.

PROLOGUE

Ten years earlier.

She propped herself up against the wall, the shadow of the bridge above shielding her from sight. Withdrawing her phone from her pocket, she pressed the button to see the time. He should be with her soon. She shuddered against the effects of the bitterly cold easterly wind that was stirring. Her heart raced when distant voices sounded at the other end of the tunnel. She scooted around the end of the wall, tucked away out of sight until the loved-up couple passed, relieved they hadn't stopped in the dark tunnel for a lustful grope. It was far too cold for that. Once they had passed, she returned to her position and waited. Memories she thought she had suppressed rose from the depths of her dark mind, a little voice instructing what she had to do to combat the torture of what the memories were putting her through.

The pub had closed its doors around fifteen minutes earlier. What was taking him so long? Finally, footsteps, a shuffling sound as if the person was staggering, finding it a struggle to stand upright, no doubt due to the alcohol they'd consumed. This had to be him. He was a drunk. Some would even say he was a borderline alcoholic, he always had been—something that repulsed her to her core. She resisted the urge to vomit when the memories emerged once more and hurriedly pushed them aside, conscious she would need a clear mind to carry out her intention.

"I knew you were waiting for me."

Making out what he'd said made her freeze. *Damn, he's spotted me.* She didn't break her cover, though, not yet. Thankfully, he drunkenly continued to slur his words as he recited the George Michael and Aretha Franklyn song, signifying that her fears had been unfounded.

His singing became louder the closer he got. She swallowed down the bile filling her throat at the thought of what she was about to do, her heart racing as she clutched the blade. She'd been over and over how this would go down, but now that crunch time was here, she questioned whether she had the balls to see it through. She had to. She shuddered at the thought of this letch clawing at her flesh. The disgusting smell of alcohol lingering on his breath as he'd tried to kiss her. She had fought hard, right up until someone had held her legs in place while the man carried out his degrading deed, stripping her of her virginity. His visits had become a regular occurrence after that first time. There was little point in her protesting. When she did, it usually ended up in her getting a slap from… She hated them both.

The plan she was destined to carry out tonight had begun to stir the second he'd laid hands on her flesh. Now, that plan was about to come to fruition, and she couldn't be happier. There was no doubting the fear touching every nerve of her body, but the eagerness to rid the world of such evil drove her on.

The footsteps came closer. He toppled into the wall around five feet from where she was hiding and rebounded off it, swiping at the air and cussing at the invisible man he believed had shoved him off balance.

What an absolute prick!

She heaved out a silent breath to calm her nerves and prepared to strike.

Four feet.

Three feet.

Two feet.

He was there, standing right in front of her. She let him pass, her nerves getting the better of her. Did she really have the courage to see her plan through? The niggling voice combatted the one urging her to end this man's life. She closed her eyes, envisaging what would happen when she attacked him. The satisfaction she would feel once the final breath left his vile body. *He deserves this!* She was doing this on behalf of the other women and children he'd raped over the years. She knew she wasn't the only one, not by a long way.

That thought urged her to break out of the shadows. She had soft-soled shoes on, so he wouldn't hear her, wouldn't know what was coming at him, not until he felt the blade at his throat.

She crept up behind him. He staggered off to the left and then took a few faltering steps to the right. Her arms outstretched, she grabbed one of his.

"What the fuck? Who's there?"

"It's me, you fucking pervert. You know what? I'm going to make you regret ever laying a finger on me, let alone shoving that smelly dick of yours inside me."

He bent his head forward, searching, trying to peer through the darkness, to see who his aggressor was.

She flung an arm around his neck and positioned the blade against his throat. His flailing arms almost sent the two of them off balance, but she held firm. She had to—there was no way she could let him go now. She had to finish the job. The first cut was always the deepest, so they said. She dug the blade into the side of his neck and wiggled it—she wanted him to feel what the sensation was like when something was forced upon him, just like she had felt in his presence over the years.

He yelled out for help.

"Shut up! Shout again, and I'll end your life here and now. I have the upper hand, remember!"

"I won't. Let me go, I'm begging you. I'll start going to church, rethink my evil ways. I'm too young to die." His words came out in one long slur.

"When? When was the first time you *raped* a woman?"

"I've never done that, I swear."

She dug the knife deep into his neck again. "Don't give me that bullshit. When?"

"I don't know. I was in my teens, I suppose."

"How many?"

"What?" he asked, leaning against her now as his legs became weak through the blood loss.

"How many women have you forced yourself upon over the years?"

He flung an arm up. "I don't frigging know. I never counted."

"You never counted the number of women whose lives you destroyed?"

"I didn't. They were up for it, most of them anyway. Most women enjoy a good shafting now and again. Admit it, go on!"

Her anger grew to another level. She couldn't stand to be near the man any longer. She placed the blade at the edge of his throat and sliced from one side to the other. He gurgled, his blood spilling over her hand. She had to force herself not to vomit. She wanted to stay there until he drew his final breath. She lowered him to the ground. His legs kicked out, and his arms flailed, but he said nothing. Within a few seconds, all his limbs came to an abrupt halt. She sank to her knees and bent close. There it was, the bastard's last breath.

Jubilation should have run through her. It didn't.

What have I done?

Her gaze darted around. Shit! Yet more footsteps approached, and the silhouette of a man came closer, his steps heavy, the sound rebounding off the underside of the tunnel roof.

She dashed for cover.

"It's no good running. I saw you."

She closed her eyes, recognising the voice of authority. *Damn! What do I do now?* There was only one thing left to do—face her accuser. Face the man who had brought this bastard into her life in the first place...

Her father.

CHAPTER 1

LORNE STRETCHED AND WINCED, forgetting for a split second the warning the doctor had given her not to extend too far or there was a possibility her wound wouldn't heal fully.

"Silly, you know what the doc told you," Tony mumbled, pulling her close for a cuddle.

She slapped his hand away. "I don't have time for this. As much as I'd love to stay in bed with you all day, some of us have work to go to."

"Cheeky mare. I have a business to wind up and packing to do if you're still serious about moving to Norfolk."

"I am. I'm only going back because Sean told me I wouldn't get paid if I didn't work my notice."

Tony chuckled. "I think you'll find he was pulling your leg. He's determined to hang on to you. Who wouldn't, given your success rate in the force? They're going to miss you when you decide to retire, Lorne."

"I know Sean better than you do, remember? I'll work the two weeks as agreed, more because I want to go out with a bang and prove to him what a great detective I am."

They both laughed.

"Deep down, he recognises that, he's just being a typical bloke, too stubborn to tell you what an asset you've been to the station over the years. I know one thing: Katy is going to miss you when you finally retire your handcuffs."

Sudden tears welled up. "I'm going to miss her, too. Sean, not so much, but don't tell him I said that. Maybe we should hold a farewell barbecue and invite all the team. What do you think? Especially as you'll be in charge of all the cooking on the day."

He squeezed her tight. "What a great idea. You'll never change, you're always thinking of others."

"Not really. There are exceptions to that. Such as when my life is in danger, hanging by a thread."

Tony grunted. "I think everyone would think the same if they found themselves in similar circumstances. I love you the way you are." He ran a gentle hand over her stomach. "Scars and all. So glad that woman didn't aim higher. You were lucky she didn't hit any major organs. My life would be a mess if you were no longer around."

She turned to face him, gathered him in her arms, and they shared a long, satisfying kiss. "We make each other's life complete. There's no doubting that, Tony. I love you more and more with each passing day."

"That makes two of us, and to think, things could have been so different for us. You hated me when we first met, as I recall."

She ran a hand through his steel-grey hair. He was ageing rapidly now, they both were, as they were nearing their fifties. "I was testing you. You were so cocksure of yourself back then, agent boy." She chuckled.

"Bloody hell, you haven't called me that in years. Can't say I've missed it."

"I remember how much those two words used to wind you up in the beginning."

"I must be getting old. I spent the best part of twenty years being an MI6 agent and I can barely remember it, or anything else come to that, before I met you."

"You say the sweetest things. That's why I love you so much. We've both led frantic work-driven lives in the past, but I feel the same way as you do. That all pales into insignificance now. It's the things we've achieved together that resonate the most in my heart and in my mind. Which reminds me, I need to get in touch with the other kennels in the area, see if they can house the dogs for a week or two until we get settled. Are you looking forward to the move?"

"Yes, except for all the packing. I think the house and land we've chosen will definitely keep us busy in our retirement."

Lorne drifted as a picture of the farmhouse with ten acres and newly built kennels flooded her mind. It was her dear friend, Sally Parker, who had stumbled across the place and emailed her the details. Lorne and Tony had shot up to Norfolk that very weekend and offered the full asking price on the property. It was as if God, or someone else—Lorne had an inkling who that was—was watching over them. They'd been exceptionally lucky selling the house and kennels they owned now. They had been snapped up by a woman in her sixties who had a similar outlook on life as Lorne. They both felt it was their destiny to save as many abused dogs as possible. Lorne's current home had turned out to be just the right size for the woman to look after on her own. Not only that, the woman, Marjorie Locksley, was a good friend of Carol's. Which meant that Carol would be sticking around for a while, to lend a hand during, and after, the takeover.

Yes, Lorne could have left the resident dogs with the new owner, but she would have missed them. So it had been agreed that Lorne would house them elsewhere for a few weeks until they had the kennels up and running at the other end, in spite of Marjorie telling her there was no need for her to do that.

"I'd better get up. Wouldn't want to give Sean an excuse to make my last two weeks at the station hell."

"I think I'll stay in bed for a while. My back's playing up from clearing all the junk out of the garage and ferrying it to the tip yesterday."

"Stay there. There's no need for you to get up yet. Want me to bring you up some coffee and toast before I leave?"

"No. I'll sort myself out later." He turned over and pulled the quilt over his head.

Lorne was ready to leave the house within thirty minutes. She'd made herself a coffee and nibbled on a slice of toast and marmalade while she took Sheba outside for her morning run in the paddock. The German Shepherd tore around, on the scent of a squirrel that had taken up residence in the large oak tree at the bottom of the orchard. Lorne whistled Sheba once she'd finished her coffee and was ready to leave.

"Come on, girl. Time to go."

Lorne drove into work with her mind racing. With all the organising to do that accompanied a house move, she hadn't really had time to consider how much she was going to miss her daughter, Charlie. She doubted that would be reciprocated, though, as Charlie was fast becoming a super police officer of her own within the K9 division. Charlie also shared a wonderful life with Brandon, her boyfriend. They had bought a small two-bedroom terraced home close to Brandon's parents and were now engaged to be married. Her heart swelled with joy. Her daughter had endured some rough times in the past and had come through the ordeal with courage and determination. She had joined the force a year earlier and had never looked back. Her colleagues respected her, but not because of who her mother was, no, they respected her due to her work ethic and her phenomenal ability to train her K9 colleagues. That was how she referred to the dogs she worked with, as her colleagues. Charlie couldn't be happier. Lorne was thrilled her life was perfect in every way. Gone were the days of Lorne fretting if she was safe.

Lorne swiped away the stray tear coursing down her cheek. She'd miss her baby, but they all had different directions to take in the future.

Katy was leaning against her car, her face tilted up to soak up the sunrays as Lorne drew into her parking space.

"Nice to see you have priorities in life, partner."

"We've got to catch the sun when we can. How are you? All ready for the onslaught of another gripping investigation?"

"Ha, as long as I don't end up being the damned victim of a weirdo. How's Georgina's teething?"

"Getting a little better. AJ is far happier now he's finally getting a good night's sleep."

Lorne smiled. "He's amazing. Not every dad would offer to put his career on hold to care for his child. So, when are you two going to be tying the knot?"

Katy sniggered. "Not yet. Anyway, the team and I have come up with a plan to keep you coming back to London."

Lorne swiped the top of her partner's arm. "I hope you're kidding. I'm going to miss you guys when we do eventually leave. You know my door will always be open to you, professionally and personally. You only have to ring me if you need my advice, and Tony and I will be disappointed if you, AJ and Georgina don't show up on our doorstep in the near future. Georgina will love the place. It comes with a small wood for her to run around in."

"To get lost in, you mean."

"That as well, I suppose. Promise me you'll come for a visit."

Katy pushed through the entrance door to the station. "I promise. Just let us know when you've settled in. We can't wait to see it. AJ has always loved the country. He was saying the other day that he's tempted to follow you."

Lorne stopped mid-stride and touched Katy's arm. "You're not winding me up, are you?"

"Hang on a sec, don't go building your hopes up. I'm still young enough to want to explore what this great city of ours has to offer."

"Yeah, but look at the long term. How much better it will be for Georgina to live in the country instead of a smog-filled city."

"Can we discuss this later? I'm in dire need of a coffee."

"All right, you win. We will revisit this conversation in the near future, though, right?"

"Yes!"

Lorne smiled, and there was a lightness in her step as they passed through the reception area. "Morning, Mick. Any news for us?"

"Nope, all quiet overnight, ma'am."

"That's great to hear."

They continued up the stairs and into the incident room. The team all stood and applauded their entrance.

"Why, thank you. But I last saw you guys on Friday," Katy announced, curtseying to the others.

Lorne chuckled. She would miss the banter within her team. "Thank you. As you were, team. Katy, why don't you grab a coffee and join me in my office, which is soon to be yours, and we'll go over the cases you've solved in the past few weeks in my absence?"

"In other words, the coffee is on me... I'll be there in a second."

Lorne sniggered and walked towards her office, pausing in the doorway to sniff the faint odour of Cool Water which greeted her. She couldn't help wondering if her former partner, Pete's spirit, would remain at the station or travel with her to Norfolk. He'd be welcome to go along for the ride.

She hadn't been at her paperwork for long when Sean Roberts appeared in the doorway. "Can I come in?"

She gestured for him to take a seat. Instead, he swept around the desk and pulled on her arm, easing her out of the chair. Then he shocked the life out of her by hugging her. Lorne wasn't sure how to react. She was genuinely taken aback by his surprise show of affection. After a few uncomfortable seconds, she wriggled free of his arms and flopped back into her chair.

Sean sniggered and sat in the chair opposite her. "Shocked you, didn't I?"

"Somewhat. I take it you missed me?"

"Yep, mostly as a friend rather than a colleague. You've been a tower of strength to me since my marriage broke up. In your absence, I've had no one who I can sound off to."

Oh crap! Yet another awkward moment coming my way by the look of things. "Sorry to hear that, Sean, can it wait?" She swept her hand over her cluttered desk. "I have this lot to catch up on, otherwise my ogre of a boss will come down heavy on me."

Sean tilted his head back and laughed. "As if I would. Come down heavy on you, I mean. You've had me wound around your little finger for years and you know it, Lorne Simpkins/Warner."

Lorne laughed. "Really? It hasn't felt like that over the years."

"I've let you get away with things that I wouldn't have let other DIs get away with, let's say that. Has Katy spoken to you yet?"

She cocked an eyebrow. "About anything in particular?"

"Taking over as DI? I wanted an insider view on how she feels about taking over the role again. I got the feeling she was doing it out of duty rather than being delighted I had offered her the job."

"No, she hasn't mentioned it. She'll give it her all, I have no doubt about that, Sean. She might need a helping hand now and again, so don't be too harsh on her to begin with."

"I'm not the arsehole you perceive me to be, Lorne. She'll be made aware that my door is permanently ajar for her."

"I told her the same thing not ten minutes ago. She can ring me for moral support whenever she likes. I have a feeling she'll be too proud to do that, though."

"Thanks, I appreciate you still offering your services. It means a lot."

"I'm sure it's going to be a struggle for me to let go, Sean. This is all I've known all my adult life. You're aware how much of my heart and soul has gone into this job over the years."

"I am, fully aware. You're the best copper I've worked with by far. I'd like to take some credit for that."

She fell back in her chair. "You're joking, right?"

He frowned. "No, not at all. I pushed you for one reason only—to make you better—and it worked. You're the top copper in the Met."

"It's all coming out now. Did you ever consider what we might have achieved together over the years if you'd been more amenable?" Her cheeks flared up when a twinkle appeared in his eyes. "Professionally," she added quickly.

"Ah, I see. There was a second there when I thought you were talking about..."

Katy wandered into the room at that moment, thankfully. She deposited two cups of coffee on the desk and left.

Lorne grabbed hers right away as her mind raced, trying to think of something to say to swiftly change the subject. She didn't want to reflect on their past, the time they had been together as a couple. That era was buried so deep in her memory bank she was determined not to let it resurface again. "Is the divorce proceeding as it should be?"

"Yes, nice change of subject there, Inspector. Don't think I hadn't noticed."

She grinned. "It's what I do best where you're concerned. Will Carmen make the divorce difficult?"

"No, we've agreed to keep things amicable for Sara's sake."

"Ha, good luck with that. Tom and I said the same, and look how that turned out."

"Have you heard from him lately?"

"I try not to bring his name up at home. Charlie loves her father and is struggling to see he's going through a rough time and yet another divorce. Life's tough for all of us. I'm so glad I finally found the love of a good man in Tony. We've been solid from the word go."

Sean nodded. "You're a perfect match. I wish I could find someone who understood me as well as he understands and loves you."

"Relax, she'll come along when you're least expecting her to, Sean, you'll see."

"I think that boat has sailed personally. I regret we didn't meet later in life. Maybe our relationship fizzled out because we were too young to handle it. Have you ever considered that?"

Her gaze dropped to her coffee cup. "Honestly? No, never. Life is for living and not for having regrets or dwelling on the past. I learnt that from my father."

"God, I miss Sam so much."

"So do I." Unexpected tears sprouted and threatened to spill. She forced them back. "He's where he wanted to be, with Mum. They were inseparable in life. He was never the same after she died."

"It's tough when you find a soulmate and lose them, so I've been told."

She glanced up. "I think I'll feel the same when Tony goes, if I outlive him, that is."

"At the hospital, he was beside himself. We all thought we'd lost you for a while there. So glad you proved us all wrong. I'm going to miss you, Lorne, more than you realise."

Katy knocked on the door and entered the room again. "Really sorry to interrupt, thought you'd want to know straight away. We've had a 'code blue' reported."

Lorne scraped back her chair and stood, a little too quickly for her wound not to rebel. "Ouch! Okay, where, and what happened? Sorry, Sean, duty calls. Maybe we can finish this conversation another time."

He stood and passed by Katy. "I would never stand in the way of an investigation, Inspector. We'll catch up later. Keep me informed."

Lorne rolled her eyes at Katy. "Thanks, that was a timely entrance. Things were starting to get uncomfortable there for a moment," she said, lowering her voice so Sean couldn't hear.

"I got the sense you needed rescuing when I dropped off the coffee earlier. Good job this call came in to save you. Shall we go? Are you in pain?"

"I'll take one of my painkillers. I should be fine in a few minutes. What have we got?"

"I'll fill you in on the way. Why don't we take my car for a change?"

"Thanks, that'd be great."

Lorne popped a pill in her mouth, washed it down with her coffee, and then left the incident room with Katy.

In the car, Katy filled her in with the details she'd been furnished with. "Control received a call from a concerned neighbour. A uniformed officer attended the man's flat and broke the door down to gain entry."

"Any reason why he did that?"

"Sorry, he said he smelt a funny smell."

"Which turned out to be the dead body, I take it?"

"That's right. SOCO are at the scene."

"Hopefully, Patti will be able to fill in the missing details once we get there."

"So, call me nosy if you like, but what was Roberts going on about?"

"Let's just say he was reminiscing over old times."

Katy took her attention off the road to look at Lorne. "You're kidding. About you and him?"

Lorne pointed at the road ahead; she'd always been a nervous passenger. "Yes, sort of. I avoided the subject where at all possible. He cottoned on to what I was doing pretty damn quickly, I can tell you. Which led to an awkward silence or two. I feel sorry he and Carmen are going through a divorce but, well, frankly, shit happens. It's called life, and we all have to deal with the problems that surface. No one said life was easy for any of us."

"That's so true. You've had your fair share of crap to deal with over the years and have come through it unscathed."

"Umm…not sure about that. My tummy would beg to differ on that one. I just hope I don't stumble across another psycho bitch within the next two weeks. They can be so much worse than most of the male criminals we hunt down."

"With one exception to that, right?"

"Ah yes, The Unicorn. How the heck does everything come back to him? I'm hoping that will change in the future. There's no reason for his name to resurface when I'm cleaning out the kennels or exercising the dogs at our new place."

Katy held one hand up and crossed her fingers. "We live in hope. How's Sean's divorce coming along?"

"We were just discussing that when you knocked on the door. It's amicable so far. I hope for his sake it remains that way."

"So do I," Katy agreed, "Otherwise I know who is going to bear the brunt of his frustration and anger."

Lorne patted her partner's knee. "You'll have to get used to his mood swings, love, just like I have over the years. Why do you think I kept my head down most of the time?"

"I'll definitely be following suit there. Ah, here we are."

They parked in a space outside the tower block of flats in a rough part of the East End. Lorne exited the car gingerly, annoyed that the painkiller she'd taken hadn't kicked in yet.

Katy spotted her wince and rushed around the car to support her.

"Don't make a fuss. I'll be fine once the tablet reaches my system."

"That should have happened by now. Maybe you need to get the doctor to up the dosage, Lorne."

"I'll give him a ring later. It's been fine at home, but then I've mostly been resting."

"I knew it was too soon for you to come back. Damn Sean Roberts!"

"Thanks for caring, Katy. Let's not make this into anything bigger than it is. We need to get up there. Let's hope the lift is working."

"You can stay in the car if it isn't. I'm not having you pass out on me."

Lorne smiled, and they set off for the communal area of the flats. Katy pressed the button to call the lift, and the doors sprang open a few seconds later. They both heaved out a relieved sigh.

"Thank God for that," Lorne muttered and stepped into the lift. The smell of urine was unbearable. "Jesus, what is wrong with people? Why piss in the lift?"

"To piss people off, I suppose. Excuse the pun. I worry about today's society, but don't get me started on the youngsters of today."

Lorne tittered. "I bet that's something your mum used to say."

Katy rolled her eyes. "More than likely. It's so disrespectful, it makes me want to haul their arses down the station and let them fester in a cell with no food and water for a week or so, see how they like living in their own filth instead of expecting others to put up with it."

"My guess is that you'd need a ginormous cell to hold the number of people concerned."

The lift juddered to a halt, and the doors opened.

They walked the length of the open-air passageway to the cordoned-off area at the end where a uniformed constable was standing guard.

Lorne and Katy flashed their IDs, and the officer raised the tape high enough for them to duck under without too much of a struggle. Katy pointed to the pile of new white paper suits lying in their wrappings on the floor. They stepped into a couple and slipped the blue covers over their shoes then entered the flat.

"Anybody here?" Lorne called as they eased their way down the cramped hallway.

"Hey, I wasn't expecting to see you. Should you be back at work yet?" Patti rushed to Lorne's side and looked her up and down. "You look pale to me. Sit down, take the weight off."

"Don't fuss. I'm fine, Patti. What have we got?"

"It ain't pretty, so if your stomach is still a bit dodgy, I wouldn't go any nearer."

"Just tell me."

"According to the neighbour, she hasn't seen the victim for four or five days. The smell in here and the state the body is in would corroborate that."

"Let's see what we have. I'm sure my stomach will cope."

Patti shrugged. "Never let it be said that I didn't warn you."

Lorne tentatively took a few steps forward, and her stomach instantly wished she hadn't. Bile rose in her throat, and she peered over her shoulder at Patti.

"I warned you, didn't I? Come on, I'll tell you what I've found. You don't need to witness it for yourself."

Katy had the sense to stay back.

Lorne returned to her position alongside her partner. "It's gross. The evidence is clear that we're dealing with a warped fucker on this one."

"I wholeheartedly agree with you. The man, Denis Tallon, according to his neighbour, was slit from his throat down his chest to his navel. I suppose they've helped me a bit there. Anyway, that's not all…"

"There's more? I didn't get that far," Lorne replied, acid burning her throat.

"Oh yes, the man's penis was cut off."

Lorne cringed and pulled a face. "Has the perp taken it as a trophy?"

Patti shook her head and returned to the body. She held up an evidence bag that she extracted from her medical case. "Here it is."

"Oh right. Do you think it was cut off as part of a torture ceremony or post-mortem?"

"I'm guessing the latter, but it's hard to say with the amount of blood loss the victim suffered from the injury to his stomach."

"Okay. What does that tell us?"

Patti shook her head again. "I haven't finished yet."

"Oh fuck. Get on with it, Patti. I'm losing the will to live here." Lorne's knees weakened; she had to dig deep to remain upright.

"I found the man's dick hanging out of his mouth."

Lorne gagged. "Oh bugger. That's awful."

"I'd say the killer was intent on sending a message, either to the police or the man's friends and family. But that's just an assumption of mine, take it or leave it."

"I'll take it. We haven't got anything else to go on at this point."

"Exactly. Anyway, I'd better crack on. The quicker we get this poor soul out of here, the more comfort the neighbours will have, knowing that we've rid them of this putrid smell."

Lorne, her stomach now slightly more settled, took a final look at the victim. She put his age at between fifty and sixty. With his stomach split open and his insides spewing out, it was hard to judge what type of build he was. In the end she plumped for on the heavier side. She glanced around the flat. By the look of things, the man lived alone as there were no, what she would call, feminine touches in the room. The coffee table was full of empty takeaway cartons, and dozens of crushed cans of lager lay beneath it.

"Looking for anything in particular?" Katy asked.

"A photo would be nice."

"Not likely to get one here, not unless he's taken a selfie on his phone. Might be worth hunting around for that."

"Good idea."

Katy went to the other end of the couch and bent down. "Here we go. Someone must have knocked it off the arm of the chair. Of course, it needs a password to open it."

"We'll ask Patti to get her team on it. Pop it in an evidence bag for me, will you?"

"I'll get the results to you ASAP," Patti shouted across the room, eavesdropping into their conversation while dealing with the corpse.

Smiling, Lorne replied, "Thanks, Patti. We'll get out of your hair now."

"I'll be in touch soon."

Lorne and Katy stripped off their protective clothing at the door and shoved it in the black bag in the hallway.

"Do you want to split up or do this together?" Katy asked.

Lorne chewed the inside of her mouth. "Together, I think. If I dry up, then you can take over."

"You won't dry up, you never have in the past."

"Glad to see you have more faith in my abilities than I do."

They walked several paces to the right, and Lorne knocked heavily on the front door of the flat. A wizened old lady opened the door and peered under the chain restraining it from opening fully.

"Yes, who are you?" She squinted at them through her large-framed spectacles as if her eyesight was rapidly deteriorating.

Lorne held her ID up in front of the woman's face, so she didn't have to strain too hard to see it. "Hello, Mrs Smithson, we're DI Lorne Warner and DS Katy Foster. Would it be all right if we come in for a chat with you?"

"Oh my, look, I don't want any trouble. I was only doing my duty by calling you."

"I quite understand. We won't take up much of your time, I promise."

"Very well. Just a moment." The woman closed the door to remove the chain and opened it wide for them to enter. "You'd better come through. I need to sit down before my legs give way; I can't stand for long. If it wasn't for that lift, I would be housebound. Bloody council couldn't give a damn. It's despicable putting old people up on this level, don't you agree?"

"I do. Shameful. Would you like me to see what I can do for you?" Lorne felt sorry for the old woman.

Katy shot her a look as if she was mad. Lorne shrugged.

The three of them took a seat in the chairs available. The furniture dated back to the sixties and had seen better days. The woman wrung her hands in her lap. A small grey pug was lying on the floor in front of a gas fire that was set on a low heat.

"There's no need for you to be nervous, Mrs Smithson, we just need to take a few details from you, that's all. Thank you for ringing us. Can you tell us when you last saw your neighbour?"

"Let me think... It's Monday now. I suppose it must have been the back end of last week, possibly Friday. That's a guess really. When you get to my age, every day seems the same."

"Okay, I don't suppose you can give me a name?"

"For him next door?"

Lorne nodded.

"He told me his name was Denis. I don't know any more than that."

"That's fine. I take it you didn't have much to do with Denis, is that correct?"

"No, Doris and I tend to keep to ourselves. I go out three times a day with her for a brief walk around the block and that's it. I come back home and shut the world out. Do you blame me with all the crimes taking place these days?"

"No, I don't blame you, although I would like to reassure you and tell you that deaths such as Denis suffered are mostly rare."

"It wasn't natural then, his death?"

"No. He's been murdered. Hence our need to have a chat with you. Can you tell us if you heard anything next door, an argument or fight perhaps?"

"Let me think...no, I can't say I did. When was this?"

"That's yet to be determined. My guess is between last Friday and today." Although she'd told the old lady that, Lorne herself put the time of the man's death closer to Friday just because of the rate at which the body was decomposing.

"Either way, I didn't hear anything. He's usually pretty good. I might hear the TV go up now and again and him shout when there's a match on, but apart from that, he's no bother. Let's hope the next person they move in there is the same. You never know, do you? I likes me peace and quiet, I do."

"Well, hopefully it'll be you who is moving before long. I have a friend on the council. I'll ring her today and see what we can sort out between us."

Mrs Smithson smiled broadly, showing off some rotting teeth at the front and the sides. "Oh my, that would be wonderful. It's such an effort for me to get out of here some days, but I have to do it for Doris's sake. She's had a mishap now and again; I can't blame her for that. My legs seize up in the morning, you see, takes a while for them to get moving. Trouble is, poor thing finds it hard to hold on for more than twelve hours."

Lorne smiled. "I'm with Doris on that one, I'd have trouble hanging on for that long, too," she joked, trying to put the woman at ease, in the hope of getting more information out of her.

"You're right. I tend to get up three or four times a night. It would be wonderful if your friend could sort out a nice bungalow with a garden for me. I don't care what area I live in. Actually, after what's happened next door, the farther I can get away from here, the better."

Lorne winked and tapped her nose. "Leave it with me. I'll have a word in her shell-like and see what we can come up with."

"You've brightened a dreary day—no, month, for me, dear. I can't thank you enough for caring about an old fuddy-duddy like me."

"Fingers crossed we can work something out for you. Going back to Denis... Do you know if he had many visitors? What about family? Did you know him well enough to ask him if he had anyone?"

"No, I haven't a clue whether he had immediate family or not. All I know is that he lived alone. Can't say I heard him have any visitors in the time he's lived here."

"How long has that been?"

"I suppose just over a year at a rough guess."

"I see. Okay, well, if there's nothing else you can help us with, then I suppose we'd better be on our way. Thanks for your help, Mrs Smithson. If you give Katy your number, I'll get my contact at the council to call you direct, how's that?"

"Oh, how wonderful."

Lorne shook the woman's hand and left Katy with her to get the details down. She made her way back to the front door and rested her forearms on the balcony, surveying the run-down area around her. *It's places like this, slums, that I won't miss when I'm frolicking around in my acreage in Norfolk.*

"Hello? I said that was a waste of time. Where were you?" Katy raised a hand. "Aww... don't tell me, you were daydreaming of pastures new, am I right?"

"Yep, we'll make an inspector of you yet." Lorne grinned and set off down the passageway. Katy trotted to keep up with her. "Let's not throw in the towel just yet, Katy. Someone must have seen something, unless the perp turned up here in the dead of night."

"Do you intend questioning everyone on this level? Is that your plan?"

Lorne stopped. Katy almost barged into the back of her. "What would you do, if you were in my shoes?"

"Okay, point taken. Ignore my griping. I'll go with the flow."

"It's called 'good intuitive policing methods', Katy. Get used to it, there's no point in cutting corners, it'll get you nowhere come the end."

Katy's eyes widened. "All right, there's no need to quote the police training module to me."

Lorne laughed. "I wasn't, merely stating facts, dear girl. Here we go. Do you want to ask the questions on this one, to give yourself more practise?"

"Now you're just being downright condescending. Are you forgetting that I used to be in your job once upon a time?" Katy huffed.

"I'm winding you up, Katy. It breaks up the day, or have you forgotten that?"

Katy glared at her and knocked three times on Denis's other neighbour's door. "If you're not careful, I'll be putting the flags up when you finally leave instead of feeling down in the mouth."

Lorne bowed her head, trying to suppress the chuckle that was building.

The door to the flat opened. A young woman holding a crying baby on her hip demanded abruptly, "Yeah, what do you want? If you're the filth, I know nothing. End of."

Lorne thrust her foot in the gap, preventing the woman from slamming the door in their faces. She showed her warrant card. "You're right, we're the filth. We'd like a word if it's not too inconvenient for you."

"It is. I have to be at the health centre for eleven. Like I said, I know nothing."

"Can we come inside?"

"What? Why? Are you going to treat me like a suspect? He was my neighbour, for fuck's sake, nothing more. I didn't even know the old codger."

"That's answered one of our questions, but we have plenty more. We can either do it here or we can do it back at the nick, it's your choice," Lorne shouted over the child's incessant crying.

The young woman flung the door back. It bashed against the wall in the hallway and half-closed again. Lorne pushed it open and followed the angry woman up the hallway and into an untidy lounge. Toys and baby's clothes were strewn everywhere. A carrier bag of used nappies sat underneath the window, and the smell was atrocious. She crossed the room and threw the window open.

"'Ere, what do you think you're doing? Close that damn thing."

Exasperated, Lorne stared at the woman in disbelief. "I can't believe the smell in here. Have you ever considered that your child might be telling you something?"

"Keep your frigging nose out of how I raise my child, or I'll report you," the young woman snapped back, clearly offended.

"Report me? For what? Caring about your child?"

"Ladies, please, why don't you both calm down? This isn't getting us anywhere," Katy intervened, standing between Lorne and the uptight woman.

"You need to tell your mate that, not me," the woman blasted.

Lorne stared at the woman, disgusted by the way she was bringing up her child. There was no need to subject the infant to such filth. It was wrong of her to be so judgemental, she knew that, but there also had to be a reason the infant was crying, almost to the point of sobbing its little heart out. In her eyes, kids of that age should be crawling across the floor in a safe environment, which this clearly wasn't. If the woman was at home with her child all day, she needed to get off her backside and care for her child properly. Her stomach clenched with anger, and she winced as the pain shot through as if she'd just touched an open live wire and received a shock.

Katy touched her arm. "Are you all right?"

"Yes, I'm fine," Lorne replied.

"Oi! It's me you should be asking that to, not her. Look, just ask your damn questions and get out of my face."

Lorne nodded at Katy to take the lead while she crossed the room and waited by the door. The young woman closed the window again as soon as Lorne moved. Her anger jumped up a notch, and she stared at the woman, wanting to make her feel uncomfortable in her own home, matching the way she was feeling right now.

"We're here to make enquiries about your neighbour, Denis. Did you know him?" Katy asked, her notebook and pen in her hand.

"Nope. Next question?"

Katy exhaled. "If you're going to be obstructive about this, Miss…?"

"It's Mrs Turner, if you must know. I ain't being obstructive in the slightest. I told you the second I opened the damn door, I know nothing."

"A few more questions, and we'll be out of your hair, I promise."

Turner flopped into the leather sofa that was cracked in numerous places. "Go on, make it quick. I have to get us both ready for our appointment."

"Okay, when was the last time you saw Denis?"

She shrugged. "Not a clue."

"This past week, in the last month?"

"Pass. Next question."

"Maybe you've either heard or seen him having visitors?" Katy asked, tapping her pen impatiently against her notebook.

"Maybe I have and maybe I haven't, I can't remember."

"It would be good if you could try and remember. This is a murder enquiry we're dealing with here, not an insignificant incident such as shoplifting."

Turner fell silent, thinking over the question, going by the expression on her face.

"Nope, nothing. Now will you leave?"

Katy sighed again. "Have you heard any shouting or any form of argument coming from his flat? It's obvious someone got in there the other day."

"Nope. How was he killed?" Turner asked, her gaze darting between Lorne and Katy.

"We're not at liberty to reveal that at this time. Do you know if the man had any relatives?"

"No, I didn't know him. Never spoken to the guy and until a few moments ago didn't even have a clue what his damn name was. Now, if you don't mind, or even if you do, I've got to get ready for my appointment."

Katy slammed her notebook shut and tucked it into her jacket pocket. She smiled tautly at the woman and turned to leave the room. "Thanks for your help," she threw over her shoulder.

"Anytime," Turner hollered back.

Lorne and Katy left the flat, the breeze of the front door being slammed gusting behind them. "What a frigging bitch. I bet she'll go to that health centre and tell them her place is spotless. I should report her. Her sort get on my bloody tits."

Katy rubbed Lorne's arm. "Calm down. She'll get what's coming to her."

"Ya think? And what'll happen to the kid in the meantime? That place was an absolute tip. I bet the kid never gets taken out to the park or anything. Her sort riles me up the wrong way." She growled and strode away, ready to knock on the next door, preparing herself for yet another barrage of abuse from the inhabitant. She definitely wouldn't miss this side of policing, not in the slightest.

The resident in the next flat was a young man. He opened the door in his boxer shorts, his hair messed up as if they had disturbed his sleep.

Lorne offered up her warrant card and introduced herself to the dazed youngster. "Is it possible for us to come in for a moment?"

He scratched the side of his face, trying to decide if it was a trick question. "I guess. Have I done something wrong?"

"We don't know, have you?" Lorne teased, smiling.

"I don't think I have."

The three of them stepped through the front door and into the lounge. Lorne was surprised to see this flat was much tidier than the one they'd just visited. "Sorry, I missed your name?"

"It's Fletch, Paul Fletcher. You can call me Fletch, though. What's this all about?"

"The gentleman two doors down, Denis, was found dead in his flat this morning. We're making general enquiries, seeing if anyone knows anything about the attack."

"Wow, poor Denis. I mean, he was a nice guy. I often had a pint with him down the pub on the corner, The Dragon's Lair."

Katy jotted down the information.

Lorne nodded. "That's interesting to know. Perhaps you can tell us if he had any relatives?"

"Nope. He told me he got divorced over twenty years ago, been by himself ever since. Said he preferred it that way, that women were like an anchor around his neck. No offence like, but I tend to agree with him."

"Thanks," Lorne replied, her tone sarcastic.

The youngster's face coloured up.

"Do you happen to know if he had a job?"

"Yes, he's a builder, or he was. Self-employed, as far as I know. He runs an ad in the local paper with his phone number and tends to do small jobs now and again. Said he was tired of working and as long as he had enough money for his rent, a few pints every night and a take-away of sorts every day, he was happy."

"I see. Did he have any visitors to the flat?"

"I don't think so. Man, I can't believe he's dead. Decent chap, he was."

"He was a regular at the pub then? Does that mean a lot of the locals will have known him down there?"

"I suppose so, although Denis tended to stick to the same crowd mostly."

"Can you give us any names?"

"I can, but they would be no use to you. I only know their first names."

"Why don't you give us those anyway and we'll do some digging back at the station?"

"All right. Mind you, you'd be better off going down the pub and seeing them yourselves. They're always down there."

"We'll do that as well, but we'll still need their names. Any idea what time they tend to meet up?"

"From around fiveish. I've finished college by then and join them for a quick half most days. Then I come back here and get on with my studies; it breaks the day up for me."

"What are you studying?" Lorne liked Fletch. He seemed a very genuine character.

"Psychology."

"What are you hoping that's going to lead to in the future?"

He shrugged. "Your guess is as good as mine. I'll probably end up stacking shelves at Tesco's or manning the pumps at a petrol station, knowing my luck."

"You will if you don't think positively about your future."

He chuckled, obviously feeling relaxed in their presence, unlike most people they interviewed regarding a murder victim. "Don't you start. I get enough grief about that off my parents. Sorry for laughing, I shouldn't be, not with Denis lying dead a few doors down. I get nervous in situations like this. Oh crap, me and my big mouth. I mean, not that I get questioned by the police a lot."

"I get your drift, don't worry. Do you have a part-time job?"

"Yep, I work at the pub most weekends, sometimes during the week if they have a function on, like a busy quiz night. It's a great place to work, if you can call it that. It's a relaxed atmosphere. The landlord, James, treats the staff as well as he treats his customers."

"That's great to know. Okay, if you can give us a list, we'll visit the pub later and try and find these people in the hope that one of them knows something."

Fletch spent the next few minutes giving Katy a number of names to jot down. They were all men, unsurprisingly, given what Fletch had said in a roundabout way about Denis not really liking women much.

"That's fantastic. We'll chase that up later. Thanks so much for your help."

They left Fletch's flat a few moments later.

"What's your take on this?" Katy asked.

"Honestly? I think we're looking at a female perp."

"Really? Ah, I get you. It's the dick being shoved in the mouth angle you're going by, right?"

"You cotton on quickly, partner. That, and from what I picked up from Fletch about the deceased not liking women."

"Did he actually make that generalisation? If he did, I must have missed it. All Fletch said was that Denis was divorced and he felt like women were an anchor around his neck."

"Okay, thanks for correcting me. I stand by what I said, though. That was twenty years ago, and he hasn't been involved with a woman since. You don't think that's strange?"

"For a man to go without sex for that long, yes, very strange. Maybe he went the other way." Lorne raised an inquisitive eyebrow. "No, I didn't mean he turned gay, far from it. What if he turned to paying for sex when he needed it? That way he wouldn't have to deal with a woman being permanently in his life."

Lorne nodded slowly. "You know what? You could well be onto something there. Okay, let's not dilly-dally, on with the next one."

"Would it be better if we split up? We'd get through them quicker. Oh, wait, silly me, no, you're not feeling a hundred percent. Forget I said anything."

"Already forgotten." Lorne grinned, covering a griping spasm in her stomach. "I'll tell you what I will do, ring the team and get them to see if Denis had a record." She contacted Karen Titchard back at the station to get the ball rolling. Then they continued along the corridor to the next flat. *Joy of joys, only six more to go!*

CHAPTER 2

SHE COULDN'T HELP IT, she was shaking from head to toe. Her father was towering over her, jabbing her with his chubby finger.

"You put your sister up to this, disobeying me like that, didn't you? There's no point denying it. I can see it in your bloody eyes, girl. Admit it, go on, I dare you."

She cowered and shook her head. *I won't admit it.* Kathryn was hungry. She'd snuck a piece of bread from the bread bin to fill the gaping hole in her sister's stomach. For a moment she thought her father was talking about something else—the fact she'd killed Denis. The fucker deserved to die, just like all the others over the years.

Her father paced the floor in front of her, invisible steam coming out of his ears. She hated him for what he'd put her through over the years. The abuse, in its many forms, had begun on the day of her seventh birthday, the day after their so-called mother left them. Deserting them, her and her sister, to seek out a better life for herself. *What kind of mother leaves her two daughters for a violent man such as my father to bring up?* If she had her way, she'd love to track down her mother through the *Long Lost Family* programme and kill the bitch. Let them find her. She'd sign up to the happy reunion, then once the cameras stopped rolling, she'd arrange to meet her mother at a secret location, tie her up and punish her daily for the rest of her life. Because at the end of the day, her mother leaving them the way she had, she'd signed them up for a life of abuse and torture. She had to be punished for that.

Despite her mother crying when she'd left and uttering the words 'I love you', nothing could be further from the truth, not in her eyes. She'd seen mothers turn up at a women's refuge centre with their kids rather than leaving them in harm's way with their fathers.

Her father swiped her around the head. "I told you to admit it. I tell you two when and what you can eat. Hear me? You have no right to eat the food I keep in this house without my damn permission. Don't think you'll get away with this either. Mark my words, you'll be punished to within an inch of your worthless, good-for-nothing life. You hear me? I've had it up to here with you and that ungrateful sister of yours." He tapped his forehead with the side of his flattened hand.

She knew how pointless it was to argue back. There was no way she was either going to admit or deny she'd stolen the food. She'd accept the punishment. It would be cruel and heartless like it always was, but she'd suffer the consequences to protect Kathryn, the same way she always had over the years. If she admitted to doing the deed, he'd more than likely keep her and her sister locked up for a week with no food, the way he usually did when they did something not to his liking. She would need to be cautious going forward. If he found out about the men, their lives wouldn't be worth living, not that they were now. She had a number of potential victims on her list; she was grateful he hadn't heard about the others she had killed over the years —after the first one, that was.

That night, ten years ago, he had discovered her under the tunnel after she'd killed Ross Collins. Realising what she'd done, against his better judgement, or so her father had told her, he'd helped her throw the man in the river after weighting him down by putting large stones inside his clothing. To her knowledge, Collins's body had never been discovered. From that night until today, her father had never let her forget what she'd done. He taunted her daily, his intention being to keep her under his thumb, doing what he ordered her to do, in and out of his bed before his impotency had struck. She hated her life. While she had the courage to seek out the other men who had raped her, she knew she would never have the balls to finish her father off for good. Why? She didn't have a clue. She knew, for her sister's sake as well as her own, she would be better off without him, but she just couldn't bring herself to do it. Maybe one day, in the not too distant future, if she was pushed far enough, that would all change. She kept a knife under her pillow just in case she ever changed her mind.

Her sister slept in the single bed next to her, in fear most nights. If anything, she should do it to protect Kathryn, just like she'd done all those years ago. However, killing their father was a different story. They relied on him to clothe and feed them. Between them, the sisters had nothing, not a solitary penny to their names. He'd ensured that over the years. He kept them imprisoned at home. The only times she had managed to get out to carry out her deeds was when her father was zonked out on his bed, drunk.

But she had plans to remedy that. She and Kathryn had been secretly working on something that would dramatically alter their lives in the future. They needed to put a few more pieces of the puzzle in place and then they would be free of this odious life. Her sister was traumatised by the plan; however, with her expert guidance, they would be celebrating their freedom soon enough.

And no, it didn't involve murdering her father. She could never do that.

Not unless she was pushed to the limit.

CHAPTER 3

LORNE PLACED her head in her hands at her desk, the sandwich she'd recently consumed playing havoc with her stomach. Indigestion had been a frequent blight on her life since her injury. She winced as yet another bout of pain scraped through her insides as if she'd eaten a dozen razor blades for lunch instead of a mere sandwich. Katy entered the office.

"My God, Lorne. What's wrong?"

She tipped her head backwards and sat back in the chair. "It'll pass. I get this after every meal. The doctor said the pain will fade over time, but fuck, it bloody hurts. I'd put it right up there with what I experienced giving birth to Charlie. You know that's why I didn't want more kids, don't you? I couldn't bear going through all that pain again, and now I'm lumbered with this retched situation."

"Shit, that's terrible. You shouldn't be here. You should go home, Lorne. Nothing is worth the pain you're going through. Look at you, you're deathly white and breaking out in a sweat."

"Let's just say that the injury combined with the damned menopause has that effect on me."

"Double whammy! My heart goes out to you. Mum's going through the menopause at present and is really suffering. She got some herbal tablets from Boots. They seem to be helping her combat the hot flushes. I'll get the name for you if you like?"

"Bloody marvellous, thanks, Katy. The doctor wanted to put me on HRT, but when he told me what the stats were for the increased risk of cancer, I backed away swiftly. Cripes, I wouldn't wish this combination on my worst enemy. Don't ever get old, love."

Katy shook her head. "I repeat, should you even be here? Let me take over the investigation while you go home to recuperate. I should stride down that corridor and give the DCI a piece of my—"

Lorne's eyes widened as DCI Roberts entered the room behind Katy.

Her partner closed her eyes and opened them again and mouthed, "He's behind me, isn't he?"

Lorne nodded, trying to suppress a smile at the colour draining from her partner's face and seemingly transferring to redden Sean's.

"You were saying, Sergeant?" He folded his arms across his puffed-out chest and glared at the back of her head.

Slowly, Katy turned to face him. "Sorry, sir. I was just venting." She pointed at Lorne. "She shouldn't be here. She's in pain and should be at home in her sickbed. I was only voicing my concern for a fellow colleague. I wasn't meaning to be disrespectful…"

"I know exactly what your aim was, Sergeant. Don't let me keep you from your work. We'll discuss this at a later time, perhaps when you don't have a murder enquiry on your hands."

"Yes, sir. Sorry, sir." Katy darted past him and closed the door behind her as she left the office.

Lorne and Sean both burst out laughing. "That was evil," she admonished him, wincing again.

Sean sat in the chair opposite her. "She's right, you shouldn't be here. You look like the walking dead."

"You were never really one to lavish me with compliments. Please don't start now, Sean. I'm fine. At least I will be once my lunch has settled."

"Do you have to contend with this after every meal?"

"Yes. Mind you, at home I can take a gentle stroll around the paddock with Sheba until the pain dies down."

He stood and walked around the desk and, placing an arm under hers, he eased her to her feet. "Come on, we're going for a walk."

"I can't, I have work to do."

"It wasn't a suggestion, Inspector, now move."

The pain instantly eased the second she got to her feet. "Yay, it's gone now. I'm all better."

He tutted. "I've warned you in the past about trying to kid a kidder, haven't I? A quick wander around the picturesque station car park will do wonders for your afternoon health."

"Picturesque station car park? Now I know you're in the throes of losing your mind."

"Whatever."

They left the office, Sean's arm tucked through Lorne's, much to her embarrassment. Katy glanced up, her expression questioning what was going on.

"The boss is taking me for a stroll around our picturesque car park —his words, not mine. As soon as I get back, I'll bring the whiteboard up to date and we'll recap what you've all managed to find out during the course of the morning."

The team kept their heads buried, but as soon as she and Sean had left the incident room, laughter broke out behind them.

"See what you've done? Made me into a laughing stock, you have. You bastard."

"I've done nothing of the sort, and that's bastard, *sir*."

"You can be such a prick at times, Sean Roberts. I'm glad I've only got two weeks to go until I see the back of you."

"You don't think I believe you, do you? I know how much you're going to miss this place and working alongside me in particular."

"Has anyone ever told you how delusional you can be at times?" She snorted, trying not to laugh at his chauvinistic ego rearing its head.

"You'll admit it when you're gone. You'll look back on your time here and regret your decision to throw in the towel early, I bet."

They reached the main entrance, ignoring the strange stares coming from behind the reception desk, from Mick and a female constable on duty.

"I bet I don't. I'm tired, Sean. Tired of life treating me cruelly. You're lucky, you've never had the misfortune of waking up in a hospital bed, not knowing if you're dead or alive. That sounds wrong; you know what I'm getting at. That situation has happened to me twice over the years, because of two crazy people, one male and one female, and to look at both of them, you would have tagged them as normal, not deranged psychopaths with an agenda. Which means that my sense of judgement where people's states of mind are concerned are wayward right now. When a major attribute like that diminishes, it's time to call it a day."

"Granted, you've been on the receiving end of a couple of awkward situations, but you've come through it, Lorne, unlike other officers who have perished in the line of duty. That proves to me the depth of your resolve. That's nothing to be sniffed at. You have to agree on that."

"Do I? My take on the situation is that I've been fortunate to escape two nutters already and the third one is likely to finish me off. Third time lucky and all that."

"That's where we differ. I always think positively about things and push aside any negativity."

Lorne came to an abrupt halt and stood there, her mouth dropping open for a few seconds. She recovered quickly to say, "What a load of bollocks you talk at times, *sir*. Off the top of my head I can recall at least a dozen instances where we've disagreed about positive and negative views on cases, or are you going to discount them?"

"You're still bloody determined to never let me win an argument, aren't you?" He sniggered, surprising her.

"You were winding me up? How could you?"

"Because I wanted to see that fighting spirit of yours show itself. I want the old Lorne back. The one who mostly couldn't give a shit what I thought. The inspector who has always been determined to get the job done whether that was with my authority or not."

"She's gone, Sean. She's buried deep within me now. Why can't you accept that and let me enjoy my retirement? I'm exhausted. Tired and frazzled beyond words. I need to feel the air around me, to care for all the abused and abandoned dogs who are relying on me to save them in this country. Let me do what I want to do without you heaping guilt on my shoulders. Will you do that?"

He shrugged. "The truth is, I'm not sure. I have my doubts that Katy is ever going to live up to your exacting standards. You can't blame me for trying to guilt-trip you into rethinking your retirement, for all our sakes."

"You're so wrong about Katy. She's filled my shoes adequately in the past, she'll do it again when I'm gone. Give her a chance, Sean."

He glanced down at his feet and scuffed the ground.

She placed a finger under his chin and forced him to look at her. "What aren't you telling me here? I know you well enough to recognise when you're keeping something from me."

"I'm being forced to reconsider offering Katy the job. The super wants me to give the position to another inspector."

Lorne gasped and ground her teeth, trying to think of the right words to say before her mouth ran away from her. "Are you kidding me? You can't go back on your word now that you've offered her the job. The frigging super needs shooting, and I'll gladly be the first in line to fucking do it. He's an utter waste of space that man, always has been and always will be. You have to fight Katy's corner on this one, Sean. You *have* to."

"Do I? I'm getting the impression that Katy doesn't really want the job. She has a young family to consider. Is it really the right step for her?"

"That never stopped me in the past. You can't be seriously doubting her abilities, not at this late stage. Fight the super on this one, otherwise I have to tell you, I think the whole team will implode. They respect Katy. No one appreciates someone new coming in and stirring things up."

"Before I do that, are you a hundred percent sure Katy wants to take over your role?"

"Yes. Oh, she might complain about it, but with her, it's all a front. You'd be foolish to pass her over for someone else, an *unknown* at that." His eyes sparkled with laughter. "Crap, are you pulling my leg?"

"Not exactly. What I'm trying to do is make you see sense. I'm forcing you to see that you still care about what happens to the team. Now that I've done that, why don't you stay? Guide this ship for years to come. If you leave now, she'll sink into oblivion, just like the Titanic."

"You're a nasty piece of work, Sean Roberts, you always have been, and I can't see that changing in the future either. Even if you did, I wouldn't be around to see it. This time, I swear to you, my resignation is final. Anyway, the forms have been sent off to complete my pension."

He cocked an eyebrow and grinned. "Have they? Would those be the same forms sitting on my desk awaiting my signature?"

Her mouth dropped open again, and her heart raced. "You bastard, are you telling me you haven't actioned them yet?"

"I might be. You'll never know."

She turned on her heel and marched back into the station, her pain forgotten as she climbed the stairs. At the top, instead of turning left to the incident room, she went right and continued to stride down the corridor. When she opened the door, Trisha, Sean's secretary, glanced up, startled by the intrusion.

"Hello, Inspector. I'm afraid DCI Roberts isn't…" her voice trailed off when Sean piled into the office behind Lorne.

By this time, Lorne had opened his door and continued her journey to his desk. It didn't take her long to find what she was looking for. She picked up a pen and ordered, "Sign it, or I'll forge your signature. Lord knows how many times I've had to do that over the years."

"What?" he cried in disbelief.

"Do it, Sean. Don't make me ring Tony and get him down here to sort you out. You know he's been biding his time on that one."

"Has he? That's news to me."

Lorne growled. "I have two words to say to you, Sean."

He smirked. "Don't tell me, the second one is *off*."

She flung her arms out to the sides and then slapped them against her thighs. "Let's just say you have a short memory. Two words: Emma Lansbury."

Embarrassment covered his features. He remained silent.

But Lorne wasn't finished with him yet. "You know, Tony and I were the only ones willing to help you when your goddaughter was kidnapped. We put Tony's life savings up for the ransom, and this is the way you treat me? You make me frigging sick! Call yourself a damn friend?" She'd had enough. If she stayed in that office a moment longer, she'd end up either giving him a black eye or kneeing him in the crotch.

She was at the door before he managed to find his voice. "I'm sorry, Lorne. You must think I'm a right shit."

"That's one word for it, although I had something far nastier going through my mind. Just sign the damn paper, Sean. Do your job, or I'll do mine and report you to the super. That's a promise, not a threat, by the way."

She heard the ruffling of paper behind her. "Here, it's done. Lorne, forgive me, our friendship means too much to me."

"Maybe you should have thought about that before. I have work to do. You've wasted enough of my valuable time already today." She stormed out of the office and found a gobsmacked Trisha sitting at her desk, staring at her.

In the hallway, she couldn't help chuckling to herself. Sean Roberts had toyed with her emotions once too often over the years. It was about time she retaliated, although she had surprised herself by the ferociousness of the attack. Her face was still flushed by the time she arrived back in the incident room. Katy glanced her way and raised a questioning eyebrow as she walked towards her. Lorne headed for the whiteboard and picked up a marker pen.

"Oh my God, look at you. Is that anger I see in your eyes? He didn't try it on with you again, did he?"

"Nope. It's not what you think. The bastard was refusing to sign off my early retirement, so I gave him a few home truths. Bugger, I didn't hold back either. I feel a right bitch now."

"Don't! I think I would have done the same if I were in your shoes. What gives him the right to try and play God with your life?"

Lorne sighed and smiled. "Thanks, partner, I needed to hear that."

"Anytime. You'll be needing a coffee to calm you down."

"I'll never say no to one of them. I'll make a start on the board."

Katy fetched the coffees and drew everyone's attention. The team gathered around, angling their chairs to face Lorne and Katy at the front of the room.

"Right, let's discuss what we've found out about the victim so far. I know it's not much, but I'd like to get it down on the board all the same. Denis Tallon was found with his intestines hanging out and other extensive injuries at his flat earlier today. His penis was dangling from his mouth." She turned to see the men in the room shift uncomfortably in their seats. "Katy and I came to the conclusion we could be looking at a female perpetrator on this one. A woman with a specific agenda in mind perhaps? What that is, we've yet to find out. I need everyone working their butts off to find out more about Denis Tallon. At the moment, it's all a little sketchy. What we do know is that he was a builder. I would probably put him down as more of an odd-job man myself. He also frequented the pub on the corner of his street daily. Katy and I will be visiting the pub later to see if we can find out more. One of the neighbours, a Paul Fletcher, told us everything we know thus far about the victim. He mentioned that he's been divorced for over twenty years and he doesn't think there has been a woman in his life since then. Personally, I find that hard to believe, therefore, we need to see if Mr Tallon had any form of record for kerb crawling. Call it a hunch, okay? Stephen, can you track down any CCTV footage around his address? Let's see if we can pick up the killer on those if possible. I've arranged the usual media conference which is due to take place within the next hour, so we'll all need to man the phones on that one. Karen, I need you to find out more about Denis Tallon, i.e. his former employers, previous address, anything along those lines. I also need you to find out if he had any family in the area. They'll need to be told, preferably before the appeal is aired. Also, look up his ex-wife, see if there are any kids and possible maintenance issues there."

Karen jotted down some notes and tapped her pen on the pad when she'd finished. "I'll get on it right away, boss."

"Anyone have any contacts on the street around that area?"

The team all shook their heads.

"That's a shame, I was hoping for a different answer on that one. Okay, anyone else got any suggestions?"

Graham raised a finger in the air. "What about a possible drug connection, boss, given the area he was found in? I know that block of flats has been highlighted for crimes of that nature recently."

"Okay, again, that's worth delving into. It might explain why a few of the neighbours weren't keen on talking to us. That reminds me, I need to get on to the council, too." She clapped to end the meeting then made her way back into her office. She lowered herself gingerly into the chair and closed her eyes briefly as a slight pain rippled through her abdomen. *Bugger, when is this pain going to bloody end? I hope it doesn't end up hampering the case.* She inhaled a large breath and rang her contact at the council. "Brenda, hi, it's Lorne Simpkins. How are you?" she asked, announcing herself to her friend with her old name so as not to confuse her.

"Hey, long time no hear. I'm fine most days. How are you? I bet Charlie is all grown up now, isn't she?"

Lorne smiled. Brenda always found it in her heart to mention Charlie. "She's twenty-two now and in the police, the K9 division, and doing really well as far as I can gather. How are your mum and dad?"

"Sadly, Dad passed away last year. Mum's declining because her heart broke when he went. It's to be expected; they were married for over fifty years. Anyway, what can I do for you? I know how busy you are."

"My condolences, I didn't know about your dad. I would have attended the funeral had I known."

"Mum didn't want a fuss. It was just family members on the day."

"Ah, I see. Sorry to hear about your mum. Tell her I said hi when you next see her."

"I will. She lives with us now. That way I can keep a closer eye on her."

"Good idea. Okay, I'm in need of a slight favour from you, if you can help out?"

"I'll do my best. I know it has to be something major for you to come knocking on my door, so to speak. What's up?"

She relayed the purpose of her call in the hope that Brenda might miraculously find more suitable accommodation for the old lady whom she'd met that morning.

"Oh gosh, that poor woman. The system really is up the creek when they assign accommodation to people of a certain age who struggle to walk. Can you leave it with me for a day or two? Hopefully I'll come back with some good news soon."

"You're a star. I can't thank you enough for this. Speak soon, I have a murderer to hunt down."

"Good luck, Lorne, it was lovely catching up, if only briefly."

"Take care, Brenda." Lorne hung up and relaxed back in her chair, a feeling of positivity shooting through her at the prospect of her old friend finding the old lady a new home soon, especially in light of what Graham had just brought up about the flats during the meeting.

Next on her agenda was to make a few notes ready for the media circus that accompanied every murder on her patch. She couldn't help wondering how many more she'd have to make before her retirement kicked in. Not many, she hoped.

She left the office forty minutes later and consulted with the team. Karen had managed to trace the ex-wife of the victim and found out that she hadn't had anything to do with Denis since they'd parted twenty years previously. She was devastated to hear about his death, sounded genuine enough to Karen not to warrant chasing her further, which was enough for Lorne. Stephen had learnt that Denis was a builder with Taylor Wimpey homes until five years earlier. Lorne shuddered, thinking about the case they had recently solved, regarding a couple of murderous builders playing havoc on their patch. "Chase that up for me, Stephen. Ask the usual questions, see if he fell out with anyone while onsite."

"Will do, boss."

"If there's nothing else, I'll see you guys in a few minutes, wish me luck." She left the incident room and descended the stairs slowly, annoyed that the old building couldn't have a lift installed. Still, a couple more weeks and it wouldn't matter to her. She entered the designated media conference room and took her seat behind the desk. She drew the journalists' attention, and the murmuring died down. She cleared her throat and announced why she had called the conference. The journalists listened patiently as she told them the facts which her team knew about the case so far, keeping from them the nature of the victim's injuries as she always did in cases such as this. Then she opened the floor up to questions.

"What was the motive, Inspector?" a young ginger-haired reporter threw at her.

"At this point, we don't know. It's still too early in our investigation for that to be highlighted yet. Next? Yes, Moira?"

"I was just going to ask if there had been any similar crimes in the area recently, Inspector Warner."

"Not with the same MO, and before you ask, no, I can't go into the gruesome way the victim died. Let's just say it wasn't pleasant. Anyone else got an important question they want to get off their chest?" Lorne asked, for some reason feeling chattier than she normally did during a conference.

The journalists bombarded her with a few sensible questions and a number of dull ones which took her around twenty minutes to answer. She rounded things up by urging the general public to step forward if they had any information about the crime or if they knew anyone associated with Denis Tallon.

Once the conference ended, she went back upstairs to the incident room. At the top of the stairs, she found Sean waiting for her.

"How did it go?" His tone was neutral, as if what had taken place between them earlier hadn't happened.

If he was willing to let bygones be bygones, then why shouldn't she? *Because he's a prick and hurt you, that's why!*

"As well as could be expected."

"Good. I've sent the form off via internal mail. It should reach them this afternoon. Sorry, Lorne."

"There's no need for you to apologise. Glad you've seen the error of your ways and done the right thing in the end. Now, if you'll excuse me, I have a killer to find."

She spun away from him. He grabbed her arm, preventing her from leaving. She glanced down at his hand until he released her.

"Can we draw a line under this, Lorne? The last thing I want is for us to part as enemies."

"So what's new there, Sean? Are you forgetting how annoyingly obstructive you've been over the years? It's only these past few years that you've treated me with any respect. You know what? I'm done with this. I have more important things to do rather than rake over old ground with you. I'll be out of your hair soon enough."

He shook his head, and his eyes watered. She soon realised she'd overstepped the mark and regretted her harsh words immediately; however, the need to voice an apology failed her. Instead, she continued her journey to the incident room and let out a relieved sigh.

"How did it go?" Katy asked.

"The usual. We've got to sit back and wait for the phones to ring now. That won't happen until later afternoon, I suspect. Have I missed anything?"

She circulated the room and gathered snippets of information from each of them. "Any luck with the CCTV footage yet?"

Stephen glanced up and made a face at her. "Sorry, boss. I couldn't get one close enough to the flats. Two streets away is the best I can do."

Lorne ran a hand over her face. "Bugger. Maybe we've come to rely too much on CCTV solving our cases recently. Okay, you tried. Don't let it get to you, Stephen."

The rest of the afternoon dragged by, with none of the information that had come their way making a jot of difference to the investigation. At five, Lorne and Katy set off, back to the murder scene, or close by at least. They dropped in to The Dragon's Lair and introduced themselves to the pub landlord.

James Marks was a man in his early forties. What remained of his hair was a light sandy colour. He greeted them with a cautious smile. "Hello, ladies, what can I do for you today?"

"We'd like a chat about one of your customers, if that's okay?"

"Fire away, I can spare you a few minutes. It's early doors yet. The locals tend to descend on us around five-thirty. What do you want to know?"

"Does the name Denis Tallon ring a bell?" Lorne asked, watching the man's reaction carefully.

"Yes, I know Denis, he's in here most days. Come to think of it, now that you mention his name, I don't think I've laid eyes on him since maybe Wednesday or Thursday of last week. What's he done? Has your lot banged him up for something?" He roared, laughing at his own inane joke.

Lorne stared at him. "Denis was found murdered in his flat today, and no, I wouldn't regard this as a laughing matter, Mr Marks, would you?"

He leaned against the bar as if needing its support. "Jesus, sorry for larking around. Of course I didn't mean anything by it. I hadn't heard about his death."

"The jungle drums a bit slow in these parts, is that what you're saying?"

"They obviously are in this instance. Murdered, you say? Why? Who did it, do you know?"

"Not yet, and the motive is unclear to us. When was the last time you saw him?"

He tutted. "Either Wednesday or Thursday, I can't be more definite than that. Apart from the weekends when we're stretched to the limits around here, every day feels the same. If it wasn't for the calendar sitting in my office and the records of the takings I keep, I wouldn't even know what month it is, let alone what day of the week it is."

"I understand. When you last saw him, was he with anyone?"

"The usual crowd. They sit at the round table over there. A couple of them are in place already—those are Len and Jeff. They'll probably be able to answer your questions more than I can."

"We'll have a chat with them in a few minutes. Did Denis ever meet up with members of the opposite sex in here?"

"Denis? With a woman? Never. He was adamant he wasn't going down that route again after one failed marriage. He always spoke disparagingly about his experience. We used to rib him, ask where he sowed his oats now. A man has got needs and all that, right?"

"If you say so, and his response was?"

"Nope. Said if he never laid eyes on another woman in this life it wouldn't bother him."

"I see. Are you saying the select group only consists of men?"

"That's right. Most of them are either married or dating someone, though Denis was the only one who was single, if I recall off the top of my head. Bloody hell, I can't believe he'll never walk through that door again. I'll miss the old fella."

"I don't suppose you have any cameras, do you? Either inside the bar or out in the car park?" She glanced around but didn't spot any.

"We have one out back, keeping an eye on the car park, none in here. Why?"

"I wondered if Denis came into contact with anyone else the last time he was in here, possibly a woman."

"Whoa! What are you saying? That a woman did this?"

"We're not sure. We can't discount any theories at this moment. Can you get us a copy of the footage from Wednesday and Thursday?"

He shook his head. "Not right now, I'm alone until the staff come in at six. I can sort it for you then."

"Okay. Would it be all right if we discreetly ask your customers a few questions?"

"Sure. Want me to announce who you are?"

Obviously, he doesn't have a clue what the word discreetly *means.*

"We'd rather you didn't. We'll just have a quiet word. Shouldn't take us long."

He nodded his acceptance and wandered up the other end of the bar to serve a customer.

"We might as well make a start with Len and Jeff."

They strode towards the two gentlemen sitting at a round table close to the door. The men shifted in their seats uncomfortably as they approached. Lorne withdrew her warrant card and sat next to one of the men while Katy sat alongside the other, blocking any possible intention they might have of taking flight.

"Evening, gents. Mind if DS Foster and I ask you a few questions?"

The man sitting next to Lorne nodded briefly. "Police? What's this about?"

"Sorry, I didn't catch your name, sir?"

"That's cos I didn't give it," he replied smartly.

The other man almost choked on the beer he'd just supped. He wiped his mouth and grinned at his mate.

"Name?" Lorne asked sharply.

Katy slapped her notebook on the table and flipped it open to a clean page.

"Len Jordache, and this is my mate, Jeff Davis. That's, I-S, not I-E-S. Make sure you jot that down correctly, miss."

"I will," Katy replied.

"Okay, Len Jordache, perhaps you can tell me when you last saw Denis Tallon?"

"Why? What's he done?"

"When was it, sir?"

He screwed up his nose as he thought. "Was it Thursday, Jeff? Darts' night?"

The other man nodded. "I think so. What's he done?"

Lorne sensed she wasn't going to get very far unless she answered their persistent question. "Unfortunately, I have some bad news for you. Denis was found dead in his flat earlier today."

Len gasped, and Jeff downed a large gulp of his bitter.

Finding his voice, Len asked, "What? Natural causes, was it?"

"Sadly not. He was murdered, hence our questions. How close were you?"

"Close enough. Good friends, we were. Jesus, I can't believe this, can you, Jeff?"

"Nope. He was always an odd chap, though, wasn't he?"

Len shrugged. "He was different, I suppose."

"In what way?" Lorne prompted.

"Always seemed a little uptight to me. Got worse when we spoke about women for some reason. I know he hated his missus, but not all women are the same, are you, ladies?"

Lorne smiled. "No, we're not. Did he ever tell you what went wrong with his marriage?"

"Not really. Avoided the subject when he could," Len replied.

"Going back to Thursday, when you last laid eyes on him, what was his mood like?"

Len placed a thumb and forefinger around his stubbly chin. "I can't say it was any different to normal."

"He didn't mention if he'd had a run-in with anyone, an argument or something along those lines?"

"No, nothing like that. Is that what you think? Someone who knew him did this to him?"

"The honest answer is we don't know. That's what we're trying to find out." Lorne sensed the men had only been drinking buddies and hadn't really known each other well at all, frustrating as that was to admit this early on in the investigation.

Another couple of men came through the front door. Len and Jeff acknowledged them as they approached the bar. Lorne noticed the men sneaking a glance their way, and after the manager had served them, the two men joined them.

"This is Tommy and Bill. Mates, these two lovely ladies are with the police. You're never going to believe what I'm gonna say next... Denis has popped his clogs," Len said.

"What? How? An accident, was it?" one of the men sporting a beard asked.

Len shook his head. "Nope, he was bumped off by all accounts."

The new arrivals drew up a couple of spare chairs and filled in the gap at the table. "No way. When?"

Lorne cleared her throat. "His body was found this morning. We're hoping someone here can throw some light on why he was attacked. Did either of you know Denis well enough for him to confide in you?"

Tommy and Bill, who both appeared equally as shocked as Len and Jeff were moments earlier, shook their heads.

"I've already told them that Denis was a strange character on occasions, that's right innit, gents?" Len took a sip of his beer.

"Why would anyone want to hurt him? He might have been a tad quiet, but I wouldn't have called him strange," one of the new arrivals said.

"Did any of you notice a stranger hanging around the pub last week?" Lorne asked, losing the will to live.

All the men shook their heads, apart from Tommy, who appeared pensive.

Lorne pounced on him. "Sir, you seem as though you've remembered something."

"I think so. When I left that night, I noticed a young girl on the corner. I might have glanced her way once or twice but I didn't like to stare. I put her down as one of those ladies of the night, if you get my drift."

"A prostitute? Would you even know what one of them looked like, Tommy?" Len ribbed the man whose cheeks flushed.

"You can be such a prick at times, Len."

"Aye, I can that."

"Sorry to break this up, gents, but we're on an urgent mission to catch a killer here."

"Sorry," Len apologised for the others.

"A young lady you said. Would you be able to give us a description?" Lorne's heart thumped against her ribcage, the way it frequently did when she felt she was closing in on a suspect.

"I don't think so. She was lurking in the shadows really. Not sure I could even tell you what the colour of her hair was, sorry."

"It was worth a shot. Did you see what happened to her? Perhaps she was waiting to be picked up."

Tommy shrugged. "I couldn't tell you, love. All I was interested in was downing my first pint."

Len sniggered until Lorne shot him a glare.

"Never mind. It's something we can look into; it's more than we had when we came in here. Is there anything else you guys think we should know before we leave?"

The four of them glanced at each other and then back at Lorne and shook their heads.

Katy flipped her notebook shut.

"Thanks for your help. I'll leave you a card. If you hear anything that you think might be of interest to me, will you ring me?"

"Sure, we'll do that, lads, won't we?" Len said, speaking up for the rest of the group again.

Lorne and Katy returned to the bar, sat on a couple of stools and waited for the owner to go over the CCTV footage with them. Finally, the cavalry arrived in the shape of two youngsters, one male and one female, who slipped behind the bar.

James Marks instructed his staff what to do then motioned for Lorne and Katy to follow him through to a cramped office which barely had room for a desk and a chair. Sitting on a shelf was a monitor, and on the screen was the pub's car park. Lorne's hopes rose a notch.

"We've established from the group of men we were just speaking to that Denis was definitely last seen on Thursday. We're also looking for a young woman who Tommy saw lurking in the shadows in the car park."

"Interesting. Let's see what we can find for you," James replied. He selected a CD and fast-forwarded through the images until the young woman came into view.

"Can you stop it there?" Lorne shuffled closer to the screen. "I can't make her out. All I can see is that she has shoulder-length hair. Looks pretty sinister to me, standing there, just waiting, either for someone to meet, or I'm inclined to think, spying on someone."

Katy nodded her agreement. "I wonder how long she stayed there."

"Let's see, shall we?" James fast-forwarded the image once again.

The woman stayed in the same position for over twenty minutes and then drifted away.

"She's leaving. I can't see anyone else around, can you?" Lorne asked, blinking a few times, her eyes sore from intently staring at the tiny screen.

"Nope, the trouble is, we can't see the main entrance to the pub from this angle," Katy said.

James tutted. "Sorry, ladies, that's as good as it gets. Do you want me to make you a copy?"

"We'd appreciate that, thanks. Looks like it's as much as were going to get." Lorne exhaled a frustrated breath and puffed out her cheeks.

Once ready, James handed Lorne a copy of the CD which she popped into her jacket pocket. She gave James a card. "Will you do me a favour and keep your ear to the ground for us?"

"I'll do that. Denis was a good man; he didn't deserve this. I hope you catch the culprit soon."

He led them back through the bar under the gaze of the customers. "Thanks, James. You've been really helpful."

On the way to the car, Lorne said, "We might as well call it a day and start anew in the morning."

"Hopefully, we'll have something more to go on once the appeal has been aired."

"I'm cream-crackered. I'll drop you back at the station and then shoot off."

"It's been a long day with nothing much to show for it so far."

"Ain't that the truth. Still, tomorrow is another day as they say."

CHAPTER 4

Lorne groaned and toppled out of bed the following morning.

"Are you all right? Say if you're not, Lorne, and I'll call in sick for you," Tony asked, concern etched into his handsome but maturing features.

"I'm fine. I just need to get moving. Don't worry about me, love. What are you up to today?"

"Packing. I seem to spend my life packing damn box after box. Are you sure we need to take all this stuff with us?"

"I've thrown out what we don't need and given a few boxes to the charity shop. The rest has to come with us."

"I think I prefer my bachelor days. When I moved from one fixed abode to another, I dumped virtually everything I owned, bunged everything else into a few suitcases and moved on."

Lorne stood at the door to the en suite and shook her head. "What about items that meant something to you? Given to you from family members et cetera?"

"Never had anything worth keeping. Maybe that's the difference between men and women."

"Maybe. I can't imagine throwing out anything that either my dad or Charlie has given me over the years, they mean too much to me."

"Men aren't as sentimental as women, I suppose. Either that or I've never been given gifts worth keeping."

"Umm...thanks."

Tony winced and tutted. "I'm talking about before I met you. I have a box of precious stuff of my own now. Damn, forget I said anything. Don't you have a job to go to?" He showed off his white teeth in a soppy grin.

"I have."

After showering, bathing her wound with more care than usual due to the shooting pains she was already experiencing so early on in the morning, she finished getting ready and joined Tony in the kitchen where he'd prepared breakfast for her.

"Gosh, you're expecting me to eat a full breakfast and then drag myself into work? I'll be falling asleep at my desk by nine o'clock. That'll go down well with Sean, not."

"I take it he's being a nightmare then?" Tony added the beans to her plate then placed it in front of her.

"Aren't you having any?" she asked, deliberately avoiding answering his question.

"I'll have something later; it'll give me an excuse to take a break from the packing."

She set down her knife and covered his hand with her own. "I'm not sure what I'd do without you in my life, Tony. Please don't ever think I'm taking you for granted."

"Where did that come from? I never think that. This is a partnership, love. One that at one point I never dreamt of having. I might complain now and again, but basically, having you in my life has made me whole. Never forget that."

"I feel the same way. Take a break from the packing for today. Why don't you take Sheba out for a visit around the lake or something along those lines? It'll do you good to have time off."

He contemplated her idea and nodded. "You know what? I think I will. I'll do half a day and then take Sheba out."

Sheba's ears pricked up at her name, and she moaned a little from her bed by the door.

"That's settled. You can't go back on your word now and upset her."

They laughed. Lorne tucked into her breakfast again and popped one of her painkillers with a mouthful of coffee.

"Is it that bad this morning?"

"It's not good," she admitted, placing another piece of Cumberland sausage into her mouth.

"I would willingly go down the station and wring Sean's neck for you."

"It's not long, Tony. I can stand the pain for that long. Anyway, I'd probably be a darn sight worse around here, hunched over and lugging boxes around all day."

"Fair comment."

She was determined not to mention that Sean had neglected in his duty to pass on her retirement form. She knew how Tony would react to that unwelcome news. She didn't keep much from her husband; however, she knew she was doing the right thing this time. Tony was a placid person until someone rattled his cage, and then he generally reverted back to his former role of tough MI6 agent, not willing to take shit from anyone, no matter what rank came before their name.

Lorne drove into work and marked another day off the calendar on her desk. Nine days and counting, if everything went according to plan.

Katy came into her office a few minutes later, waving a note in her hand. "We might have something here."

Lorne sat back in her chair and placed her hands over her slightly bulging tummy. "What's that? To do with the case, I'm guessing."

"We've had a call from a distant relative, says she's Denis's niece, an Emma Chadwick."

Lorne sprang upright in her chair and got to her feet. "Ouch, I shouldn't have done that. Remind me I have to do things slowly and rein in my excitement for now. We should get over there and see her."

"We should. Are you sure you're up to this? I can take one of the others with me, if you'd rather stay here."

Lorne eyed her as if she'd just been released from a straitjacket.

"Umm...no. I'm going, and that's the end of it. Where are we heading?"

"An address near Rickmansworth."

"Ah, Hertfordshire. It'll be nice to get away from the city for a few hours."

"Want me to drive?"

"That'll make a change, which means I can enjoy the scenery this beautiful country has to offer."

Katy shook her head. "A tad over the top."

"I take it Emma is expecting us?"

"She is, in half an hour."

"I hope the traffic is in our favour then."

THEY ARRIVED at Emma's tiny terraced house five minutes later than anticipated. Lorne rang the bell.

A nervous-looking brunette with highlighted blonde strands opened the door. "Are you who I spoke to earlier?"

Lorne nodded, and she and Katy both showed their ID.

"DI Lorne Warner, and my partner DS Katy Foster."

"You'd better come in. I've been pacing the floor since I made the call, unsure whether I'd done the right thing in ringing you. Do you want a drink?" Emma led them through to the tiniest lounge Lorne had ever seen. The whole house appeared to be of doll's house proportions.

"No, we're fine. Why, are you having second thoughts, Emma?"

Emma glanced over to the right to gaze out of the window. She scratched both sides of her neck until she had created red patches and then looked back at Lorne. "I'm not sure where I should begin."

Lorne motioned for the nervous young woman to take a seat. "Please, try and relax. Do you know something about Denis's death, is that what this is all about?"

Emma collapsed into the grey velour sofa and placed one of the mustard-coloured cushions in front of her, crushing it with her arm. "No, the first I heard about his death was when I saw it on the news.

Until then I'd tried my hardest to forget all about the wretched man."

Lorne shot a glance at Katy who raised an inquisitive eyebrow. "Are you saying you didn't get on with your uncle?"

"Please, don't call him that. I hated him."

"Okay, can you tell us why? Take your time, I can see how upsetting this is for you."

"It is. He was a callous man. Yes, that's the word I would use for him, bloody callous."

Lorne and Katy sat in the sofa opposite. "In your own time, there's no rush. Can you tell us why you'd say that about your… umm…Denis?"

"Everyone thought he was such a genuine man—he wasn't. He was a monster. A wolf in sheep's clothing, if you like."

Katy jotted down some notes. Lorne nodded at Emma to continue without interrupting her.

Emma stopped talking, her gaze darting around the room as if trying to latch on to something that could possibly calm her while she spoke.

"You're all right, Emma, you're safe now. Please, what did he do to you?" Lorne had an inkling what Emma was about to reveal and suspected it wasn't going to be pretty. So much for Denis being well-liked at his local. Over the years she'd discovered the many faces people hid behind and placed Denis Tallon in that category, without Emma even telling her what he'd done.

Silent tears rolled down the young woman's face, and she did nothing to wipe them away. "I'm sorry. This is so hard. I haven't thought about this stuff in years. I thought I had successfully locked it away. Oh God, it's all come flooding back. Why? How could an uncle betray the trust?"

Lorne left her seat and sat on the arm of the chair close to Emma. She placed a hand over hers. "When did it start, Emma, the abuse?"

Emma turned her head to face Lorne. She looked bewildered beyond words. "You know? What it's like to be abused?"

"Not personally, but I've dealt with plenty of people in a similar situation as yours in the past. Have you had any counselling?"

"No. I couldn't bear the thought of reliving the details over and over again. I've blocked it out all these years. I refused to let him control me even when I'd banned him from my life."

"I can understand that. I hear it a lot, Emma. What age were you?"

Emma gulped loudly as fresh tears fell onto her cheeks. "How could someone abuse the trust? A family member who my parents trusted? I was five when it first began. I didn't know what was happening to me. He told me he loved me…" Her voice drifted off.

Tears threatened to spill from Lorne's eyes. She tilted her head to the ceiling as if to stem the flow. "I'm sorry. Did your parents know?"

Emma shook her head. "No. I refused to tell them. I should have… maybe if I had, the abuse would have stopped. He was my dad's only brother. Dad loved him, had cared for him when they were growing up because their parents had died in a car crash when Dad was only sixteen."

"That's no excuse for what he did to you. Was it just you whom he abused, or did he do it to other members of your family?"

"I don't know. If he did it to me then I'm sure he was doing it to others. I can't be sure of that, though. I've kept the secret from my parents for so long, I can't tell them, not now he's dead. I should feel better now, yes? Instead, the image of him lying on top of me, crushing me under his weight, is constantly in my head. As I got older, he must have sensed that I wanted to tell my parents. To keep me quiet, he used to tell me that he would rape and kill my mother."

"That's awful. I'm sorry this has brought all those vile images back, Emma, my heart goes out to you. Maybe you should find the courage to tell your parents now that your uncle has passed away."

"I couldn't, it would kill Dad. He idolised his brother. Brought him into our home when his luck was down. That's when the abuse started…"

"That's a lot for you to contend with, I'm sorry. Maybe you should consider seeing a therapist."

"I couldn't live through the ordeal again, I just couldn't. I hated him. I'm not sorry he's dead. Sorry if that makes me sound a terrible person, but it's the truth."

"It doesn't. I totally understand the hatred you must feel inside."

"Who did it? Killed him, do you know?"

"Not yet. We suspect the perpetrator might be a woman. I know it's a long shot, but did you know any of your uncle's friends, former girlfriends perhaps?"

She shook her head slowly. "Why do you believe it was a woman?"

"Certain details that have come to our attention."

Emma chewed her lower lip. "You don't think he abused other little girls, do you?"

"There's no telling if that's true or not. Do you think he did? Can you remember any other children being around during your childhood?"

"No, only me. Maybe he regarded me as easy pickings." Emma closed her eyes and shuddered.

"Possibly. Are you up to telling me how long the abuse lasted?"

"Until I was sixteen. I left home then and refused to have any contact with him after that. I haven't heard or seen him for years. To me he was dead anyway. Maybe it's relief I'm feeling now. Relief that he'll never force himself on me again."

"I reckon. I hate to ask this, but do you think he would have attacked other children in your neighbourhood? Perhaps children living next door? Did you ever hear any gossip along those lines?"

She thought the question over for several minutes. "No, I don't think so. Oh, I don't know. Maybe if he did, the kids were too scared to speak out, like me."

Lorne sighed, suddenly grateful for coming from a family where love meant that she was truly loved for all the right reasons and wasn't tainted with any form of abuse. "Do your parents live locally?"

"Yes, although they're away on a cruise around the Caribbean at the moment. Oh God, how the hell am I going to break the news to Dad? I've been so wrapped up in my own debilitating memories that I've completely forgotten that I'll need to tell them."

"Would you rather we broke the news to them?"

"Would you? Perhaps I can pretend I didn't know. Wait, they might learn that I contacted you and then…oh dear, what to do for the best? That damn man is still causing turmoil even though he's dead. Sorry, I didn't mean to speak ill of the dead, it's just…"

"You don't have to apologise to us. We quite understand what you must be going through. If you can keep up the pretence, then I'll willingly contact your parents for you. I'll obviously need the details of their trip."

"Dad's pretty cute, he'll know that you got the details from me." Emma's concern was etched deep into her features.

"I can say we kept the reason why we needed their travel itinerary from you. Which will keep you in the clear. Where there's a will…"

A relieved smile spread Emma's lips apart briefly. "Thank you."

"Is there anyone you'd like us to call? A friend or another member of your family perhaps?"

"No, there's no one. I'll give Mum and Dad a huge hug when they come home. That usually puts things back into perspective for me."

"I hate to ask, but do you have any background information you can share with us about Denis? We know he was a builder, doing odd jobs here and there for beer money, but what we don't know is any personal stuff, apart from the fact that he divorced his wife twenty years ago. Did they have any kids?"

"No, thank God. I think that's why the relationship broke down. He was desperate to have them; she had problems conceiving. I can't help thinking what a blessing that was. Otherwise the child would have lived a life of abuse, right?"

"I'm inclined to agree with you on that one. Girlfriends since his divorce?"

She shook her head. "Honestly, I wouldn't know. I cut him out of my life years ago and did everything I could to avoid him. Dad invited Denis over to the house several times a year. I made sure I came up with a plausible excuse not to join them every single time."

"That must have been so hard for you, given how much you adore your father."

"It was. I hated hurting Dad like that, but it was the lesser of the two evils, I suppose. Lord knows what I would have done if I'd been forced to sit around the dining table with that *man*."

"Let's hope the memories begin to fade now that he's gone."

"I hope so. They've been pushed back for so many years. Is there anything else you need from me? Only I'm due at work in an hour."

Lorne smiled. "I think that's all. What type of work do you do?"

A proud smile appeared. "I work with abused children. It's truly helped me cope with the situation. Some of these kids went through so much more than I did when I was younger, not that it's a competition, of course. Every abused child deserves to know that what they've suffered isn't the norm in this world. Like I said before, over the years I've managed to push the memories aside. I believe working with children less fortunate than me has allowed me to do that. Some of these children were abused by their parents—they're in the system now. They'll never know the true meaning of 'family love'. Knowing that has helped me cope over the years. Maybe I'm wrong thinking of it in those terms. I consider myself lucky that my uncle only managed to abuse me periodically. Some of these kids were raped by their own mothers and fathers every day of their short lives. You can't imagine what they have to contend with emotionally. Not every child can successfully block out the images as I have in the past."

A ripple of emotion ran the length of Lorne's spine. "That's horrendous, to know there are parents out there willing to treat their children so appallingly."

"You'd be surprised. I dealt with a whole family of kids a few years back. There were ten of them. Their mother hated every one of those kids, abused them every day of their lives, either mentally or physically. When she was finally arrested, she told the police the only reason she had so many kids was to take her pain and anguish out on them. Every single one of those kids had a different bloody father."

Lorne ran a hand over her face as an angry flush filled her cheeks. "That's sickening. People like that deserve the death sentence. Those kids will spend the rest of their lives not trusting people, I'm guessing."

"That's where we come in. We try to right the wrongs in their eyes. Show them that what they were subjected to wasn't love. Some of them understand while others sink further into their shells. It's easier to work with the younger children who are just confused. The older children bear so many scars, as I did. I've come to realise over time that what I suffered at the hands of my warped uncle was nothing in comparison. I'll go back to work today and forget all about what he did to me. I have to, so that I can try to heal other children."

Lorne squeezed Emma's hand. "You're a special lady. I hope the healing you dish out to others heals you eventually."

Emma smiled. "I'll get there. I think it's going to be far easier now that I know my abuser will be rotting in a grave soon. Sorry if that sounds harsh and cruel. They say you have to walk a mile in someone's shoes to truly appreciate what that person has gone through in life."

"That's so true. I can tell you're a strong woman, Emma. You'll get past this; don't let it eat you up inside."

"I try not to. I've learnt to appreciate life more nowadays, that's for sure. I'll teach the kids in my care that true love does exist for them. While I'm doing that it'll hopefully help me to forget what happened in my own past."

Lorne stood and handed Emma a card. "Ring me if you need me or if you hear of anything you think we should be interested in. Take care, Emma."

Katy tucked her notebook in her pocket and joined Lorne at the door.

Emma nodded, and a glimmer of a smile appeared on her pale face. "Thank you. Good luck with your investigation. I feel like telling you to pat the person who killed Denis on the back for me, but that would only make me look bad in your eyes."

Lorne touched her arm. "You have every reason to think that way in the circumstances."

Emma closed the door behind them.

Once they were back in the car, Lorne let out a long sigh. "That was tough. I'd feel the same way if I were in her shoes. How can you feel sympathy for a man who abused you from such a young age? Who threatened to kill your mother, if ever you opened your mouth?"

"Okay, I'm throwing this out there because, well, basically we have got fuck all else to go on right now…"

Lorne swivelled in her seat to face Katy. "Go on."

"What if her parents found out and they're behind Denis's murder?"

"You heard what she said, they're on a cruise. Do you have any idea how far away the Caribbean is, Katy?"

Katy sighed and clenched her fist. "That was below the belt, even for you, Lorne. Of course I'm aware of how far the Caribbean is. What does that matter? If they found out about the abuse, they could have paid someone to bump Denis off." Katy folded her arms. "We've come across something along those lines in the past, even you have to admit that."

"Don't get in a tizzy. Okay, let's note it down when we return to the station. We'll need to carry out background checks on both the mother and father. My take is that we won't find anything relating to his family. If he abused Emma, then the likelihood of him abusing other children is very high indeed. That's the avenue we should be going down. Christ, if he abused his own niece, then what's to stop him doing the same thing to dozens of other children?"

"Let's not get carried away. Emma said her father took Denis in for a while. Maybe he seized the opportunity and couldn't stop abusing her once he'd started." Katy held up a finger. "I'm not making excuses for him, I'm stating facts. Maybe he didn't go on to abuse other children when he left their home and moved on."

Lorne leant over the steering wheel and glanced up at the sky. "Wow, that flying pig has the curliest tail I've ever seen."

Katy slapped her arm. "Mock me all you like, odds are that we're not going to get to the bottom of it anyway."

"Now that's you talking sense. It's going to be a tough case to solve, there's no doubt about that."

"You still reckon it's a woman though, right?"

"Yep, intuition is telling me that a man wouldn't cut another man's dick off."

Katy sniggered. "I take it you've never seen *Game of Thrones* then?"

Lorne's brow furrowed. "That's a fantasy-based series, isn't it?"

Katy laughed. "Whatever. If ever you get the chance to see it from the beginning, I'd watch it if I were you. All I'm saying is the murderers we deal with are bloody angels compared to that mob."

"Crikey, and there was me thinking it was all about dragons and shit like that."

Katy chuckled as Lorne started the engine and did a three-point turn in the road.

CHAPTER 5

THE GIRLS SAT HUDDLED on the bed, Kathryn's teeth chattering. Claire hated seeing her sister so scared. That was why she had to change things. It hurt her heart and her soul to witness the trauma her kid sister was going through. She'd always protected Kathryn and she had no intention of letting her sister down now that they were so much older.

She had more courage in her little finger than her father gave her credit for. In his eyes, she was weak, except on that one occasion when he'd caught her killing Ross Collins. She shuddered at the thought of him discovering her that evening. She'd dropped her guard, her mind set on killing Ross and disposing of his body. She'd almost died of a heart attack when he'd emerged from the shadows, demanding to know what she was doing.

Claire tiptoed across the room and opened the door. This door was never locked, they were never sure why, but their father kept the front door locked at all times and hid the key. She knew where the key was hidden and was determined to sneak out of the house while he was passed out on the sofa in the lounge, the TV blaring, disguising any noise she might make in the process. They could have left years ago, but without funds it would be difficult for her and her sister to survive. That would be remedied soon enough. Like most abused victims, they can see the light at the end of a distant tunnel but are unable to move towards it without having a plan in place and the money to fund their escape.

"I think he's asleep now or should I say passed out? Either way, I'm going to make my move."

Kathryn flew off the bed and landed at Claire's feet. "Take me with you. Please don't leave me here alone with him. What if he wakes up? Where should I tell him you've gone? I'm confused, Claire. I don't want to do this any more. Let's steal his stash of cash and get the hell out of here."

"Where would we go? He doesn't have that much money, love. I have a plan, let me do things my way."

Kathryn shook her head, and her eyes watered. "At what cost? If you kill all these men then you're no better than them, Claire. What will I do if they catch you? Can you imagine the punishment Dad will mete out then?"

Claire sank to the floor and cuddled her sister. "You have to remain strong. This is our only way out."

"It's not and you know it. Why not kill father and be done with it? It would free us once and for all. Then we could live here, try to pick up the pieces and move on with our lives."

The thought of killing her own father had never sat comfortably with her. She couldn't explain why. Perhaps he had some form of psychological hold over her, something that was hard to explain, even to her own sister.

She tugged Kathryn to her feet and settled her on the bed. "Stay there. I'll check to see if he's asleep yet." Claire opened the door slowly, praying it wouldn't squeak after she'd put some WD40 on the hinges the previous day. She wandered down the stairs, keeping to the edges of each step, and poked her head around the door to the lounge. Her father was in his usual position, lying on his back, his mouth open wide, a spilt can of lager on the floor by his side. She made her way back up the stairs to their room. "He's asleep. I'm going now. I shouldn't be too long."

"What if he wakes up and discovers that you're missing?"

"Pretend you were asleep and tell him you have no idea where I am. Don't fight me on this, Kathryn. I have to do this, for both our sakes."

Her sister laid down and gathered the pillow in front of her, looking like a scared child. Claire pecked her on the forehead and removed her jacket from the hook on the back of the door. She crept down the stairs and collected a chair from the kitchen table. On the high shelf, to the right of the front door, her father had placed the key. She gathered the key and returned the chair to the kitchen. Claire snuck out of the front door and quietly closed it behind her.

She sprinted down the street and caught the bus into town. She had a list of men she wanted to kill. Claire ran her finger down the list and chose Larry Small. She knew he owned a betting shop in town. She was taking a risk going there at this time of night, but she'd heard her father mention to a mate of his over the phone that he knew Larry often worked until ten or eleven at night. She prayed this was one of those nights. The bus dropped her off around ten minutes later. She glanced up at the church opposite—it would be striking ten o'clock soon. Claire decided to see if Larry's car was parked in the alley at the back of the shop. It was—at least she thought it was his. She hunkered down next to a commercial-sized wheelie bin and waited.

She didn't have to wait long. Larry appeared in the doorway, a holdall in his right hand. He secured the back door to the premises and whistled gaily as he walked towards his Audi. Her heart rate spiralled, and she had to talk herself out of backing down. She had to do this, for Kathryn, and for herself.

Claire swiftly closed in on him, as quick as a cheetah hunting down its prey. Within seconds she was behind him with a knife to his throat.

"What the...? The money is in the bag, take it...don't hurt me, please. I have a wife and two kids."

"Boys or girls?" Claire demanded, gruffly, disguising her voice even though it had been years since he'd last laid a hand on her.

"What? Why? Please, leave them out of this. Take the money...I promise not to report you to the police. I'll keep schtum, you have my word."

She snatched the car keys from his raised hand.

"Take the money and the car. I don't care about material things."

"You didn't answer me, boys or girls?"

"Boys. Please, leave my family out of this."

"Why should I? They have a right to know what kind of despicable animal their father is."

He tried to turn around, but the knife nicked his throat. "Ouch! What do you mean? I'm not an animal."

"Aren't you? Why don't I give you a few seconds to rethink your answer? Think long and hard, back fifteen years ago."

Larry gulped. It was obvious he'd remembered. "I didn't mean…I don't know what you're talking about," he corrected himself.

She dug the knife deeper into his throat.

"All right, I remember, I'm sorry for lying. I'm sorry for everything. Please, it was a long time ago. I'm happy now. I have a young family of my own."

"Maybe I'll pay your sons a visit. Sneak into their room in the dead of night and rape them, like you did to me. Yes?"

He gulped again and sobbed. "I'm sorry. I was foolish then. Young and foolish. Please, please forgive me. I didn't mean to do that to you. I've regretted my actions ever since that night. I was drunk. Your father dared me."

"I'm well aware of what happened, I was there, listening to your disgusting conversation. The way you treated me was barbaric. No child should be subjected to such deplorable actions. How would you feel if the same thing happened to your sons? Boys can get raped as well as girls, or do you draw the line at that?"

"I would never hurt my sons, they mean the world to me."

"I want you to know that once I kill you, I'm going to pay your wife and sons a visit and kill them as well. Rid the world of the evilness that you may have passed on in your genes."

His elbow struck her in the face. He cried out for help and ran to the end of the alley. Ignoring the pain and the blood erupting from her nose, she bolted after him and launched herself at his back. She plunged the knife between his shoulder blades. He cried out and dropped to the ground with her on top of him at the edge of the alley.

Over and over she stabbed him. Initially, he cried out during the attack, but towards the end his cries for help and forgiveness receded. She'd had enough and decided to give his throat a permanent smile. She placed a hand over his nose. No breath—he was dead. Jumping to her feet, she dragged his body to one side of the alley. However, she wasn't finished with him yet. She undid his belt and trousers and tugged them down. Then she sliced off his dick and placed the flaccid part in his mouth before the rigidity in his body crept in.

On her journey to the car, she dumped the bloody knife in the bin. She was wearing gloves anyway, so even if the police discovered it, they'd have a job being able to trace it back to her. She started the engine. It had been a while since she'd driven, her father had allowed her to take lessons just in case anything drastic happened to him. At first, the car was an untamed beast in her hands, until she got used to the feel of it on the open road. Claire drove around town and avoided drawing any attention to herself by sticking to the speed limit. She passed several cameras on the side of the road, but she was safe. Used to disguising herself over the years, she'd wrapped a scarf around the bottom half of her face; there was no way anyone would be able to make out who was driving the car if they spotted her on the cameras.

Ten minutes later, she headed back towards the house. Dumping the car at a disused warehouse close to her home, she snatched the bag off the back seat and ran the rest of the way home. She eased the front door open. Her father's snoring drifting from the lounge forced out a sigh of relief from her. She locked the door and carried out the same ritual of fetching the chair from the kitchen to replace the key in its hiding place. Then, with the holdall in her hand, she snuck up the stairs again. *I have to hide this money! It could be the one thing that saves us in the end.* She glanced up at the hatch in the hallway. Dare she put it in the loft? Would the risk of waking her father be worth it?

She decided it would. Her father had an old kitchen chair in his bedroom, so she crept in there to collect it and placed it underneath the hatch, then opened the loft door. She squeezed the bag past the ladder and secured the door again.

"What are you doing?"

Claire's heart skipped several beats. "Jesus, Kathryn, you scared the crap out of me. Go back in the bedroom, I won't be long."

After returning the chair to its rightful place in her father's bedroom, Claire had a quick wash in the bathroom and joined her sister. She undressed quickly, slipped on her pyjamas and jumped into bed beside Kathryn.

"What were you doing?"

"Securing our future."

"What's that supposed to mean? Why can't you just be straight with me for a change? Why do you insist on having secrets all the time?"

"Because I don't want to worry you, love. Trust me. I have everything in hand. The less you know, the better."

"Better for whom? Me or you?"

"Kathryn, don't do this. I've told you before, everything I have ever done has been for you."

"I don't want that burden on my shoulders. It's for us, not just me."

"Of course it is. Now, let's get some sleep, I'm exhausted."

"Why? What have you done?" Kathryn asked, sounding exasperated.

"Hush now." Claire pulled her sister tighter and kissed her cheek. *All will be revealed soon enough.*

CHAPTER 6

Lorne had a weird sensation running through her on the journey into the station that morning.

"Morning, Lorne. Is everything all right?" Katy was just getting out of her car when she drew up alongside her.

"I'm not sure. Something is playing havoc with my insides."

"You mean from the injury?"

"No. Oh, I don't know. Maybe I need a couple of cups of coffee to settle my nerves. How's Georgina? Did you manage to get any sleep?"

"She was crawling around the living room floor last night when I got home. AJ said she'd been a nightmare all day and wanted to wear her out before he attempted to put her to bed. It seemed to do the trick, not a peep out of her all night. It's heaven managing to get eight hours kip now and then. It definitely sets one up for the day. This is the best I've felt in weeks."

"That's wonderful news. Long may it continue. Now you know why there are all these adventure play parks around for the kids. Might be worth AJ taking her to one of those places a few times a week."

"I said the same thing. I'm all for having a quiet life. Anyway, how did this conversation turn away from you? How are you feeling in yourself?"

They locked both cars and walked through the main entrance to the station.

"I'm all right. At least the pain in my stomach has subsided a little. I did take an extra dose of painkillers at seven this morning. I hate taking the damn things, but they seem to keep the pain at bay for a while."

"That's a relief. You looked like shit yesterday. I was too scared to tell you in case you snapped my head off."

Lorne placed a hand over her chest. "What? Moi? Never."

They both laughed and ascended the stairs, Lorne setting the pace.

"So what's this feeling you've got? To do with the case?"

"I reckon. We'll have to wait and see what develops this morning. Obviously, there's been nothing overnight, otherwise Mick would have said something on the way in."

"That's a good thing. I much prefer to ease myself into the day rather than get a callout first thing to attend to."

"Me, too. Shit happens at times, though." Lorne pushed open the swing door to the incident room and switched on the light.

Katy walked towards the vending machine, turning on the computers on the team's desks as she went.

Lorne paused at the whiteboard to appraise what they'd gathered so far about Denis Tallon's death. The truth was, very little. The previous afternoon, after the revelation had come out from his niece, Emma, that he'd abused her from an early age, the investigation had switched directions slightly. They needed to dip further into Denis's past to see what they could dig up about any probable links to child pornography sites or a possible paedophile ring. Lorne shuddered at the thought. These types of crimes had always appalled her, since her own daughter had suffered at the hands of The Unicorn. Thankfully, Charlie had emerged from her ordeal a courageous and well-balanced young lady, which was a huge relief to both of them.

Now Charlie was working alongside her, well, sort of. Working at the same station as a police officer. Although she was involved in the

K9 division of the force, Lorne had a sneaky suspicion that she would move on from that role soon. She had high hopes that one day her daughter would fill her shoes and run the team she would be leaving in less than eight days.

"Penny for them?" Katy startled her. She held out a cup.

"Gosh, scare the shit out of me, why don't you?"

Katy bit her lip. "Sorry."

Lorne waved away her apology and perched on the desk behind her. "I was just thinking, daydreaming if you like."

"I thought you were, about your retirement?"

"Yes and no. What Charlie was subjected to in the past has reared its ugly head again, as it often does in child abuse cases. I know it's a different scenario, but as a mother it still hits the same heartbreaking spot."

"Had you told me that a few years ago, I would have thought you were nuts, but now that I have a child of my own to protect, I totally respect where you're coming from. The saving grace is that Charlie appears to have forgotten her past—that's an observation from an outsider, of course. I'm not sure many young women would have been capable of doing that if they'd walked in her shoes during that terrible time."

"I'm super proud of her achievements and the way she's dealt with her life so far. If she was showing any signs of struggling then I wouldn't be moving out of the area and starting a new life elsewhere."

"Do you think Charlie will follow you? Let me rephrase that, are you hoping she will?"

"Honestly? I haven't considered it. She has her own life to lead with Brandon now. He's a genuinely nice lad, so I know she'll be in safe hands."

"That's lovely to hear. It must be a load off your mind, too."

"It is. Right, time to start the day proper as it were. I'll be doing my usual of trawling through the mundane paperwork. Now that's one job I'm particularly looking forward to passing over to you."

"And the one job I'm having cold sweats thinking about doing *every* damn day."

Lorne chuckled and walked into her office. She hadn't been sitting at her desk long when the phone rang. "DI Warner."

"Sorry to interrupt, ma'am, I thought you'd want to know about this one right away."

"Oh dear, that sounds ominous, Mick. Let me get a pen and paper."

"Rightio. A chap just rung us to say he found his boss in an alley behind the betting shop he owned."

"Okay, I take it his boss is dead, right?"

"Damn, yes, that's right. The thing is, ma'am, the man's penis was cut off."

Lorne looked up, her gaze locking on to a plane passing her window. "Wow, okay. Katy and I will shoot over there now. Give me the address, Mick. I take it SOCO and the pathologist have been informed?"

"They're at the scene now."

After noting down the address, Lorne ended the call and shot out of her chair. "Katy, grab your jacket. We've got another one."

"Another what? Murder?"

Lorne nodded. "Yep. Same MO, too."

"Ouch," Graham muttered as Lorne swept past him.

"Keep doing the necessary digging into Denis Tallon's past, folks. Don't forget to delve into Emma's parents' pasts as well, just in case something shows up there. We can't discount anything at this point. Katy and I will be back soon, I hope."

LORNE LET Katy drive to the location. They ducked under the crime scene tape after showing their IDs to the constable guarding the scene.

Once they were suited and booted in their protective clothing, Lorne and Katy approached the crime scene. Lorne stood behind Patti who was kneeling, examining the victim.

"Hey, what have we got?"

Patti glanced up and flashed a taut smile. "A dead body missing his tadger."

"Crikey, I haven't heard that term in a while. Was it removed pre- or post-mortem?"

"Post, I believe. But fear not, we have found the missing part." Patti held up an evidence bag containing the body part.

"Okay, are you going to tell us where it was found?"

"In his mouth. Not poking out of his mouth like the previous one, no, this one was shoved inside. And they say size doesn't matter," Patti added drolly.

Lorne chuckled and rolled her eyes. "You're a nightmare. Would you be making jokes if you were a male?"

"Probably." Patti grinned. "Lighten up. This has been the highlight of a miserable day for me, don't put a damper on it."

"Whatever. Where did all the blood come from?" Lorne was looking over the victim's body. The blood was mostly staining the ground around the man's head.

Patti pulled on the victim's shoulder, and Lorne spotted the large slit in the man's throat.

"He went out with an extra smile to when he entered the world then," Lorne noted.

"You could say that. I'm taking a wild stab at this and suggesting this case is linked to the victim we have sitting in the fridge back at the lab."

"I sort of came to the same conclusion." She scanned the surrounding area. "Any weapon found?"

"Nothing yet. By the size of the wound, I'm guessing a large kitchen knife was used."

"Maybe it's around here somewhere."

"I've got my men searching the area. I'll give you a shout if we find anything."

"I need to have a chat with the guy who reported the incident. Have you seen him?"

"He's inside. Told me he needed a brandy to steady his nerves. I hope he hasn't gone over the top and isn't tanked."

"So do I. We'll leave our suits over there and put them on again once we've finished with him."

"Good idea. I'll carry on here and speak to you soon."

Lorne and Katy disrobed and walked around the corner to the front of the shop. It was closed. Lorne knocked on the window. A man in his early thirties peered around an internal door. Lorne flashed her warrant card at him. He rushed to the front door and invited them in.

"Hello there. DI Lorne Warner, and this is my partner, DS Katy Foster."

"Hi, I'm Jack Drew. I was the one who found him and rang you guys. Bloody hell, it was such a shock to find him lying there like that."

"You look shaken up. Would you prefer to do this in the office?"

"Yes, I need another shot of brandy. I'm trying to pluck up the courage to ring Susie, his wife."

"There's no need for you to do that. We'll handle that side of things, if you can give us his wife's address and phone number."

"Phew, that would be a load off my mind. I wouldn't know where to begin. I suppose you guys must be used to that."

"We are. It's not easy for us either. People react differently when they hear the news. Can you tell us a bit about the deceased?"

"Larry Small, he's owned this business for around ten years now, I think."

"Is it a busy betting shop?" Lorne asked while Katy jotted down the information.

"It has its moments. Depends if there are any major sporting events on, such as the World Cup in football and rugby. They're the real money spinners for us."

"Can you recall Larry mentioning if he'd had any kind of problems with a punter recently?"

"We get the odd spat with the customers, but nothing that would warrant one of them wanting to kill him. I'm shocked this has happened. I've always regarded Larry as a decent chap, who is, sorry was, devoted to his family. Shit, I think you need to tell Susie quickly. I saw a bloody nosy reporter and a photographer hanging around before you showed up."

"We'll pay her a visit shortly after we've spoken to you. Can you tell me if you get many women punters placing bets with you?"

"Sometimes. I suppose it would work out that women are around five percent of our trade."

"I see. Did you know much about Larry's personal life?"

"Such as what?"

Lorne shrugged. "Was he the type to have an affair?"

"No way. As I told you, Larry was devoted to his family. He's got two little boys, Gary and Zac. He idolised those kids, spent every spare moment with his family."

"Do you have CCTV cameras on the premises?"

Jack hit the side of his head with his fist. "Why didn't I think of that?" He rushed out of the office, and Lorne heard boxes being moved in the room next door. "In here, if you want to take a look."

Lorne and Katy marched up the corridor to find him.

"There. This was when Larry was locking up the shop. It was around ten o'clock."

"Did he always leave so late?"

"No. We generally get away around six-thirty. Now and then he'd stay behind and do his accounts, he told Susie not to expect him home until late. Damn, I wish I'd stayed with him now. Maybe he'd still be alive."

"Possibly. We'll never know the answer to that. Can you recall anyone losing their temper with Larry over the past few weeks?"

"No, nothing along those lines. Maybe it's because my mind is all over the place right now."

Lorne produced a business card from her pocket. "You can ring me if you think of anything in the next day or so. There are only internal cameras, no external ones?"

"No, Larry said he couldn't afford to fork out for them. Nothing much happens outside anyway. We usually keep the cars in the alley, and that's about it."

"I don't remember seeing any cars parked out there today, or were they moved before we got here?"

"I parked across the road. I panicked when I saw Larry lying there."

"I see. What about Larry's car?"

He covered his eyes with his right hand. "Damn, I never thought of that. I'm such a dickhead. Larry's car isn't here."

Adrenaline pumped through Lorne's veins. Something to go on at last. "What make is it?"

"An Audi Quattro. Black. I can give you the reg if that'll help? What am I saying? Of course it will bloody help you."

He reeled off the registration number, and Katy noted it down.

"Is there anything else you believe we should know about? What about takings? What happens to those at the end of the night?"

"Larry usually deposits them at the night safe a few days a week. He was due to do that last night."

"Roughly how much takings are we talking about?"

"A couple of days' money would equate to around twenty grand, I'm guessing. If I can find the accounts, I can give you a definitive answer." He went back into the office and returned a few minutes later with a green accounts book in his hands. He tilted it towards Lorne for her to read for herself.

"Just over twenty-five thousand. So this could be a robbery after all."

Katy shook her head slowly. "You're forgetting the victim's injuries."

"Yep, only for a moment, thanks for the reminder."

"Am I missing something?" Jack asked, his brow rippled with creases.

"We have an ongoing investigation we believe this could be related to," Lorne explained.

"Whoa, are you saying Larry was killed by a serial killer?"

"Possibly. We won't know that until the forensic team have completed their tasks. One last thing, we'll need Larry's address. That'll be our next stop, to visit his wife."

"Of course, want me to write it down for you?"

"If you could."

Jack handed Lorne the details, and she and Katy left the shop and returned to the crime scene. Patti was standing alongside one of her team close to the large red Biffa wheelie bin. Lorne and Katy slipped back into the white suits and approached them.

"Looks like you've found something," Lorne said.

Patti held up an evidence bag containing a large knife. "Matt found it in the bin."

"Is it too much to ask if there are any prints on it?"

"I can't see any. We'll examine it thoroughly back at the lab. How did you get on?"

"Okay, if he hadn't had a body part cut off, we would be going down a robbery gone wrong route."

"Much money taken?"

"Twenty-five grand, give or take a couple of hundred."

"Interesting."

"You could say that. Right, we're off. Get the reports to me on both victims ASAP, please, Patti."

"I will. Good luck," Patti called after them.

Back in the car while Katy drove, Lorne rang the station. "Graham, do me a favour and run a check on this reg: LAR69. It's a black Audi Quattro belonging to a Larry Small. We believe the killer stole his vehicle. Katy and I are on the way to break the news to the wife now. Get back to me as soon as you locate it, will you?"

"Of course, boss. Leave it with me."

Lorne ended the call and leaned back against the headrest.

Katy turned to face her briefly. "Are you all right?"

"Yep, just thinking. You know what this means, don't you?"

"What?"

"The killer has a wad of money that would enable them to get away before we have a chance to track them down."

"I was thinking along the same lines, unless…"

"Unless?"

Katy shrugged. "I'm just thinking about the frequency of the murders. What if the killer has an agenda, some form of list they're working their way through?"

"You could be right. Let's hope Graham can pick up the car off the

ANPRs. It's going to make our lives a lot easier. At the moment, we've got shit all to go on."

"There's the knife. Maybe that will turn up something."

"I doubt it," Lorne's response was downbeat.

"Hey, don't do that."

"Do what?"

Katy sighed. "Get downhearted. I know you're coming up to retirement, but this is so unlike you. You're the most positive person I know when dealing with shits like this."

Lorne smiled. "I know. This feels different to me. Maybe it's the abuse angle that's getting me down. I don't know."

"Meaning what? That you're empathising with the killer?"

Lorne faced Katy, who by the tone of her voice, sounded shocked by Lorne's revelation. "I stated that I couldn't put my finger on it. Blimey, it would take a lot for an abused woman to do what she's doing, right? What if she is working her way down a list? That means that she was likely abused over and over by these men. How would you deal with that?"

"Jesus, Lorne, don't put that on me. She's murdered two people that we're aware of. How many other bodies are lying out there waiting to be discovered?"

"We could say that about every victim we find, Katy, but we don't. I don't know what I'm trying to say here. Yes, I do. We could be dealing with a female perpetrator who is on the edge. You know as well as I do what that could mean."

"Either she's going to kill the men involved or kill herself."

"Exactly. Our quandary is what we're going to do about it."

"We need to dig into each of the men's past and see what comes up. There has to be something linking the two men. Who knows how many more bodies are going to show up? For all we know this could be the end of it."

"You're right, we're clueless at this stage. Maybe the perp will take the money and run now. She's taken Larry's vehicle, maybe she has contacts willing to supply her false plates. That side of things would be easy enough to achieve, wouldn't it?"

Katy let out a large breath. "I suppose so. The truth is, we don't know when the likely abuse took place. Going by what Emma told us about Denis, he last abused her over ten years ago. Maybe he mended his ways since then."

"Hmm...and Larry is married with two kids of his own, not that it means anything. He could have a sideline his wife doesn't know about."

"I admit this is a tough case that isn't making much sense at the moment. Let's see what Larry's wife has to say about things, then get back to the station to do some brainstorming with the rest of the gang."

"I agree." Lorne fell silent, contemplating the killer's motives and their possible agenda for the rest of the journey as she glanced out of the window.

Twenty minutes later, they parked in front of a detached house in a select street on the outskirts of the city. Lorne whistled when she studied the huge house. "The betting business obviously does well by the look of this place."

"I think you could be spot on there," Katy replied, getting out of the car.

They walked up the path to the house. The front garden was edged in low-clipped hedges. In the centre of the lawn, on each side of the path, was a flower bed brimming with a cascade of flowering shrubs and perennial plants. Lorne admired the planting and pondered if she'd have time to take up gardening when she retired. *Possibly not, given that my intention is to rescue all the stray and needy dogs in the area. Retirement? What retirement?*

"Hello, are you still with me, Lorne?"

She smiled at her partner. "Sorry, I was miles away."

"No shit, Sherlock! I said, do you want me to handle this or do you want to take the lead?"

"I'll do it." She rang the bell, and they waited several seconds for the door to be answered.

A young blonde woman filled the doorway. She frowned when she saw them and closed the door slightly. "Yes, what do you want?" she demanded.

Lorne produced her ID and held it up for her to read. "Mrs Small? Would it be okay for us to come in?"

Her hand automatically flew up to cover her mouth. "Oh my God, it's Larry, isn't it?"

Lorne nodded. "It would be better if we did this inside."

The door eased open. The woman appeared dazed as she stepped back in the large hallway. Over in one corner was a grand oak staircase which had glass panels at the side instead of spindles.

"What is it? Is he in hospital? He didn't come home last night. I've tried ringing him, but his phone went to voicemail all the time. Oh God!"

"Maybe we should speak about this in the lounge?" Lorne suggested.

The woman nodded and led them through the hallway into a large open-plan living room. The farthest end of the room was dominated by a white glossy kitchen with wooden worktops. The centre part of the room contained the dining area, housing a vast table and twelve chairs. Mrs Small sat on one of the four leather sofas in the lounge area.

She motioned for Katy and Lorne to sit opposite her. "Please, just get to the point. I need to know what's happened to him."

Inhaling a large breath, Lorne said, "It is with regret that I'm here to tell you that your husband died last night."

Mrs Small let out a deafening scream and fell back on the sofa, her eyes wide until she covered them with her heavily jewelled hands.

Lorne and Katy glanced at each other and then back at the distraught woman. Lorne was in two minds whether to cross the room and sit next to Mrs Small or not. She hadn't really come across as the warm fuzzy type.

They left her to cry for several minutes until she flew upright in her chair and demanded, "What happened? How did he die?"

"We're not sure how the incident occurred just yet. Your husband was found behind his business premises this morning by one of his employees."

"Oh my gosh, are you saying he'd been there all night, even while I was trying to ring him?"

"It looks that way. We've seen the CCTV footage. Apparently your husband left the shop around ten."

"He rang me at eight-thirty, told me he was thinking of leaving soon, then he discovered another pile of receipts that he'd not accounted for. I presumed that he was working later to put everything in order. And all the time he was…dead. Oh, shit! What about the boys? They're going to be mortified about this. What am I saying? I'm mortified. We had so many plans we wanted to fulfil in the future, and now…" Tears dragged the mascara down her cheeks. "How? How did it happen? Was it his heart? He's been a little stressed lately. You know what it's like when you're self-employed and running a business. This damn uncertainty about Brexit isn't bloody helping either. Our takings have halved in the last year or so. We've had to tighten our belts around here. This place is on the market. We're going to have to downsize…"

"I'm sorry to hear that you've been having money troubles lately. Umm…sorry to have to inform you that your husband was murdered."

"What?" Mrs Small screeched and then sobbed, rocking back and forth in her chair.

Lorne decided to approach her. The woman must have felt her sit beside her and flew into Lorne's arms. It was several minutes later before she pulled away again and wiped her blackened eyes on a tissue.

"Are you all right? Maybe we should call a relative to come and be with you."

"My family disowned me when I married Larry."

That snippet of information piqued Lorne's interest. "I'm sorry to hear that. May I ask why?"

Mrs Small shrugged. "I don't know. Actually, I do. They're snobs, and Larry has a bit of a past."

"Care to tell me what kind of past?"

"He was mixing with the wrong crowd at one time."

"Doing what exactly?" Lorne pressed.

"He wouldn't go into detail. Always told me that he regretted the things he'd done in the past and that he was eager to have children with me and to start afresh."

"I see. How many children do you have?"

"Two boys, six and eight. He idolised them. Gave them the world. Oh my, I'm not sure what we're going to do without him. Financially, I mean."

"You'll need to speak with his solicitor with regard to a will or see if he had a life insurance policy in place."

"I'll do that now," she said, wiping her eyes on the back of her hand, momentarily forgetting her grief.

Lorne resisted the urge to shake her head at the woman's switch in character. It was clear Mrs Small was only concerned with the materialistic side of life and lacked any empathy for human life, her *husband's* life. "If you wouldn't mind waiting until we leave, I have a few more questions I'd like to ask you first."

"Oh yes. How silly of me. I apologise, my mind is all over the place. What sort of questions?" She blew her nose on a fresh tissue.

"Perhaps you can tell us if Larry had any problems with anyone lately?"

She instantly shook her head, not bothering to take her time to consider the question. "Nope."

"Going back to what you said earlier, about Larry's past, perhaps you can give us a few names from the old days?"

"Nope. He never told me any. He didn't even tell me what problems he had back then. I tried to get it out of him, but he clammed up every time I mentioned it. He told me he'd moved on and preferred not to live in the past."

"Could one of his friends know the details?"

"He doesn't have any friends. He said that's the way he preferred it, just me and the boys. And now he's gone, and I'm left alone with the boys. How the hell am I going to cope? Oh crap, does this mean I'll have to run the business?"

Lorne hitched up her shoulders. "I'm presuming so. Maybe you could ask Jack to manage the place for you while you make the arrangements for your husband's funeral."

"What? I have to do that as well? Don't the authorities do that in instances such as this?"

"No. It's the responsibility of the family to bury their relatives, that's the way people prefer it to be." Lorne's frustrations went up a notch.

"That will mean a lot of running around for me to do. Oh heck, I haven't got a car, we had to sell it last month. But wait, what about Larry's car? Was that at work?"

"No, we believe the perpetrator took it. My team are trying to locate it as we speak."

"Well, I hope I get it back soon, not that it's ours anyway, it's on finance. The only thing that belongs to us is the number plate. I bought it for Larry a few years ago for a birthday present. I was in a dilemma; what do you buy a man who has everything? I knew he'd always wanted one. Cost me a packet, that did. I want it back ASAP, can you do that?"

"As I've already said, my team are trying to find it now. There's also something else I should tell you."

She frowned and stared at Lorne. "Go on."

"Your husband left with the takings from the shop. Unfortunately, the bag holding the takings was missing from the crime scene."

She gasped. "No! What a bastard, is that why he was killed?"

"Possibly. We've yet to determine what the motive is. We're doing our best to find out, but it's proving difficult."

"Why?" Mrs Small asked angrily.

"Well, these things take time. We came here as soon as Jack gave us your address. However, in light of what you've shared with us today, we're no further forward than when we left the crime scene. Does your husband have an office at home?"

"Yes, he has a study upstairs. Why?"

"Would it be possible to have a rummage in the office? Maybe we'll find something in there that he was determined to keep from you with regard to his past."

Mrs Small narrowed her eyes. "Don't you need a warrant for that type of thing?"

"Ordinarily, yes. However, if you want to find out who did this to your husband, I'm asking that you work with us on this one."

"Whatever. I don't care about his past. All I'm interested in is what happens to me and my boys now that he's dead. I know I'm going to struggle. Can't you give me some guidance? Put me in touch with someone who can tell me what to do next?"

"It's not our responsibility to do that, to be honest. Our role is to investigate the murder and try to bring the perpetrator to justice as swiftly as possible."

"But I'm lost. I don't know how to move forward," Mrs Small whined.

Lorne saw Katy get her mobile out of her pocket and tap the screen. "I have the number for the Citizens Advice Bureau for you. I'm sure they'll help you if your solicitor can't."

"Can you write that down for me? Thanks, I appreciate it."

Katy scribbled the number down, tore off the sheet and handed it to the woman.

Lorne stood and walked towards the door. "Can you tell me where the study is?"

"Upstairs, the second door on the right. I don't think it's locked."

Katy followed Lorne up the grand staircase.

"Thanks for giving her the number; she was ticking me off. I hate it when people expect you to do everything for them."

"Play nice, Lorne, she's just lost her husband, for fuck's sake," Katy whispered, glancing back over her shoulder in case the woman had followed them.

"I know. She just rubbed me up the wrong way when she dismissed her grief and homed in on her future. Genuine people don't do that within minutes of learning about their spouse's death."

"That's true. Let's forget about that and concentrate on the task in hand."

"Here it is. What's the betting it's locked?" Lorne tried the handle and breathed out a sigh of relief when the door opened.

They entered the room which was surprisingly tidy. It was dominated by a large mahogany desk. Around the room were several matching bookcases, filled with text books and literary fiction, along with several knick-knacks which Lorne presumed his wife had bought Larry as gifts over the years.

"Why don't you take that end of the bookcase and we'll meet in the middle?"

"Mind telling me what I'm searching for?" Katy asked, appearing to be daunted by the task ahead of her.

"A notebook, a list, anything along those lines."

"We could be here all day."

"Stop complaining and get on with it." Lorne extracted the first book from the shelf and held it upside down by the front cover. Nothing fell out, so she moved on to the next book. Katy followed suit, and between them they searched the entire library of books within half an hour. "Nothing."

Katy swivelled away from the shelves and stared at the desk. "You're missing the most obvious hiding place, surely."

"Ya think? That's why I deliberately didn't search there first. Let's have a look."

Lorne crossed the room and opened the first drawer. There was nothing in there apart from pens and other forms of stationery items such as paperclips et cetera. Katy got down on her knees beside her.

"What the heck are you doing?"

"Bear with me." She stuck her head under the desk.

Lorne heard something being torn from the wood, and her partner emerged holding a small book in her hand.

"Methinks this guy has been watching too much TV."

"Clever dick. He's not the only one, eh?"

Katy grinned and handed the book to Lorne.

Opening the first page she was confronted by a list of men's names. "Bingo. You've found it."

Katy glanced towards the door and lowered her voice. "Are we going to take it without telling her or what?"

"I can't do that. You know I prefer to do things by the book. We'll shove it in an evidence bag and tell her."

"What if she asks what it is?"

"Then we'll say it's a list of business contacts who we need to get in touch with to interview and promise to bring the book back in a few days."

"Let's hope that works."

"It will. She's too preoccupied with her own future to worry about this. Let's get back to base."

Lorne removed an evidence bag from her jacket pocket and slipped the notebook inside. Mrs Small was pacing the hallway at the bottom of the stairs. She looked up, her gaze immediately drawn to the bag Lorne was holding by her side.

She pointed and asked, "What's that?"

"Information that we need to look into. A list of associates we're keen to interview. We'll return it in a few days."

Mrs Small nodded, seemingly satisfied with the response. "Is that it? Are you done now?"

"For now, yes. We appreciate you letting us have a snoop around. We'll be in touch soon, hopefully once we've caught the culprit."

"Good. I hope you find them soon. I want to know why they did it. Why they decided to strip this family of my dear husband, the father of my children."

"We'll find out, you have my word on that, I promise."

BACK AT THE STATION, Lorne brought the team up to date. Actually, they all had information to share that proved interesting.

Graham had successfully traced the vehicle and sent a patrol car to search the area where the ANPR cameras had last spotted it. The patrol team discovered the vehicle within fifteen minutes of beginning their search. It had been abandoned by the killer and was en route to the forensic lab for them to examine.

"What about the driver, Graham? Could you make out who was driving the car?"

He turned to face his screen. "This is all we have, boss."

Lorne joined him and peered over his shoulder. "Damn and blast. She or he has a scarf around their face. I'm still inclined to believe it's a woman we're after." She filled the team in on what they'd found at the crime scene, the knife in the bin and the injuries the victim had suffered before and possibly after his death. Then she went on to reveal the book they had discovered at the victim's house. Holding the evidence bag up, she announced, "This little book I feel is going to be the key to solving this case—at least I hope it will be. Want to know where my suspicions are leading me?" It was a rhetorical question. Lorne continued quickly. "My take is we're going to stumble upon a paedophile ring."

Katy's hand swept over her pale face. "God, I hope not. There's no telling how I'm going to react if we trace the rest of the men in that book."

"I know what you mean, partner. We're going to have to be professional about this. We need to track these men down before the killer homes in on them."

Karen cleared her throat to speak. Lorne nodded for her to go ahead.

"I did some digging on Larry Small while you were out. Fifteen years ago, he was arrested for kerb crawling and for having sex with an underage girl. She was fifteen at the time."

"It would appear that Larry wasn't as innocent as his wife painted him to be," Lorne stated.

"Do you think the wife knew?"

"I'm not sure. I'd like to think not. Thankfully, the man has two boys of his own and no girls. I dread to think what that family would have gone through if he'd had daughters." She shuddered at the thought. "Okay, Katy, you and I will work on the list. I need everyone else to keep digging with regard to background checks et cetera.

Stephen, I'd like you to get the financial side of things nailed down for me. See if there are any large amounts of cash being moved around between the victim's personal accounts. Give me a lowdown on how Larry's business was doing as well while you're at it."

Katy bought everyone a cup of coffee and joined Lorne in her office a little while later. Together they went through the list of names, securing the men's likely addresses. The next step was to trace any possible convictions for them.

Two of the men had attempted rape charges to their names and had spent the minimal derisory sentence in prison for their crimes. Lorne was interested in speaking with those men first.

"Are we going to do it today or leave it until tomorrow?" Katy took a sip from her coffee.

"I'd love to do it today but I'm knackered. Let's leave it until tomorrow and call it a day."

"I'm all for that. Maybe the killer will strike again tonight and save us a job. Oh shit! Did I really say that out loud?"

Lorne chuckled. "You're a wicked woman, DS Katy Foster, even though I'm inclined to agree with you. Paedophiles are the lowest of the low in this universe. They deserve everything they get and more sometimes."

CHAPTER 7

When Lorne arrived home that evening, her stomach was telling her she'd overdone it. Tony was in the kitchen, preparing their meal.

"Hello, love. Crap, you look like shit."

He left the pot he was stirring and rushed to help her, guiding her to a seat at the table.

"Sorry, I was fine on the drive home. I got out of the car, and my stomach was on fire. I'll be all right in a bit."

"Have you had a painkiller recently?"

"Lunchtime, I think. You know how it is, you think you've taken one and end up forgetting."

Tony reached for the tablets lying in the middle of the table and placed the box in front of her, then filled a glass with water from the tap. "Drink this. When are you going to learn to look after yourself properly?"

"Aww...I do, Tony. Don't have a go, love. I'm tired."

He placed his hands on either side of her face and kissed her gently on the lips. "I'm only looking out for you. You shouldn't be back at work. I should bloody come down that station and give Sean a piece of my mind."

"Eight more days, and I'll be free. Don't get angry, love. It's wasted energy. There's nothing we can do about it, so what's the point? How have you got on today?"

"All the spare rooms and most of the master bedroom are now packed up." He raised a hand to prevent her from talking. "Don't worry, I've not taped up any of the boxes yet in case you need to get to anything."

"You know me so well. Sod's law that we'll need something in an emergency. That's always happened to me in the past." She placed a hand on his cheek. "You spoil me. You're such a treasure. Most men would probably make up one feeble excuse after another to get out of the packing."

"What have I told you over the years? I'm not most men. I appreciate how hard you work and I'm willing to pull my weight, I always have done."

"You have. I love you so much, Tony. What's for dinner?"

"Stir-fry vegetables and a chicken kiev."

"Yum, do you want me to taste the stir-fry? I know how difficult it is to get the flavours right."

Tony laughed and helped her to her feet. "In other words, you don't trust me on that score."

Lorne took a spoon from the drawer nearest the stove and tasted the sauce. She mulled it over for a little while and realised that there was indeed something missing from the mix. She then opened the larder cupboard, selected the oyster sauce and waved the bottle at Tony.

"Damn, I knew I'd miss something out. You're amazing to have detected that."

"It's not only at work where my detective skills come in handy. I'll add a splash and finish off the dinner, if you want. My pain is dying down now."

"If you're sure. I haven't taken Sheba out for a while; she could do with a run in the paddock for ten minutes."

"Go. Leave this to me."

He pecked her on the cheek and patted Sheba on the head. "Come on, girl. Let's go find your ball or chase some squirrels."

Lorne slipped off her jacket, put it on the back of a chair and returned to the stove. The vegetables still needed another five minutes cooking. She stirred them constantly in the sauce and checked on the kievs in the oven. To her amazement, Tony had prepared homemade kievs which looked good enough to eat, rather than resorting to the processed junk available in the supermarkets nowadays. She smiled, thinking back to his first attempt at cooking, when he'd placed dried spaghetti, without any water, in her expensive copper-bottom pot and ruined it. He'd definitely come a long way since then, thankfully. Even though he did most of the cooking, she still liked to keep her hand in and preferred to cook the meals herself on her days off. Most people found cooking stressful, but not Lorne. It was a form of relaxation therapy in her eyes, except when she'd been training Tony. Those days had been some of the most stressful of her life in the kitchen.

Tony entered the back door as she was dishing up. "Great timing as usual," he said smugly. "That's Sheba knackered for the night."

"I'll tell you what, once all this mess is cleared up, we're both going to veg out in front of the TV. We deserve a night off."

"I agree. Fancy a glass of wine with your meal?"

"I'll give it a miss."

"Sorry, I forgot about your painkillers. Okay, OJ it is for both of us then."

"Don't be an idiot. You have one, it won't bother me."

He grinned and saw to the drinks. Once the meals were plated, Lorne placed them on the kitchen table.

"How was work?" he asked.

"So-so. It's early days yet. Another murder happened overnight, same MO. The victim's penis was cut off."

"Ugh...now that piece of news could have definitely waited until after we'd eaten."

"Sorry, I didn't think."

"What's your gut instinct telling you?"

Lorne finished her mouthful of chicken and took a sip of juice. "That we're looking at a spate of revenge killings. The evidence is minimal at present, but so far it's highlighting a possible paedophile ring."

Tony grunted. "I'm saying nothing. You know my thoughts about people with that despicable trait running through their genes."

Lorne covered his hand with hers. "Yep, I feel the same way. It doesn't mean I'll treat the investigation any different to how I would normally."

"I don't know how you do it."

"That's the thing, I don't have to do it for much longer, love."

Tony raised his glass and clinked it against hers. "Thank God for that. We're both getting too old for this shit!"

They both laughed and completed their meal whilst discussing what lay ahead of them over the coming few months.

"I'm so glad to have you by my side for this amazing adventure, Tony."

"As opposed to Tom?"

"He would never have agreed to the move. He was always stubborn, dug his heels in a lot whenever I suggested anything. Take this place, for instance. He would never have agreed to run a kennel. Whereas you, even with your background of travelling the world as an undercover agent, you had no objections at all. You're one in a million, Tony. I'm thankful every day for having you in my life."

"You're getting soppy in your old age, love."

"Maybe I am. Maybe I just appreciate the people around me more than I have done in the past. I'll be sad when it comes to saying goodbye to Charlie and Carol." Tears misted her eyes. Feeling foolish, she swiped them away.

"They'll visit often, I have no doubt about that."

"I hope so. Fancy some ice cream? The kievs were superb by the way, you clever man."

"There, I thought I'd surprise you with my skill."

"You did that."

They cleared the table between them, washed and dried the dishes then took their bowl of salted caramel ice cream into the lounge.

"Fancy watching a film?"

"Why not? Hopefully I'll keep my eyes open until the end."

Tony popped a DVD in the machine, but before the credits had a chance to roll, the house phone rang. Lorne was the closest and answered it, preparing herself for bad news. "Hello."

"How's my best friend getting on with her packing?"

"Sally, how the devil are you? No kidding, I was going to ring you at the weekend."

Her old friend chuckled. "I've saved you a job. Are you almost ready for the big move?"

"Tony has been an angel. He's supervising that side of things. I'd say he's fifty percent there."

"Why aren't you doing it? Oh wait, that was a dumb question, given your injury. You should be taking care of yourself. I'm glad Tony is on hand to help you. You've got a good'un there."

"I can vouch for that. I'm at work for the next eight days, and yes, I'm counting down the days."

"What? Are you insane?"

"Nope. My DCI pulled a fast one, told me he wouldn't allow me sick pay if I didn't show up for work."

"Wow, Sean must really want to hang on to you. That's crap, though. I'm afraid I would've told him where to stick his job. You're still recovering from your operation. What if you have a relapse?"

"I'm taking it easy, I promise. Katy is doing a lot of the heavy lifting as it were at work." She had to bite her tongue, keeping the fact that Sean hadn't actioned her pension a secret, with Tony present.

"What a way to treat a serving officer of your calibre. That DCI of yours needs stringing up. I'll volunteer to do it if I'm ever down that way. Hugs to you, hon. Do you even have the time to get excited about the move?"

"Yes, I'm finding the time to have the odd daydream, my partner will attest to that, although the latest investigation we're dealing with is a tad gruesome."

"Eww...please don't go into details. I hated working on the gruesome cases, much prefer dealing with cold cases these days."

"Each to their own. I think I'd find them frustrating, and let's face it, there's enough frustration flying around when dealing with a case committed the week before, let alone investigating one that happened decades earlier."

"It took a while to get used to, but now I enjoy it. Maybe when you move, you can pay me a visit at the station, help out on a case or two?"

"Get out of here. What part of the concept of taking early retirement don't you understand?"

"It was worth a try. I really enjoyed working on that case with you a few years ago."

"Is that bitch still trying everything she can to get out of prison?"

"Yep, her appeals keep getting thrown out, I'm pleased to say. She's manipulated one man too many over the years. Last I heard was that prison life didn't agree with her and she was ageing rapidly."

"It couldn't happen to a nicer person. The way that woman ruled her daughters, forced them to do her dirty work for her...well, I'm not even going to go there. Evil bitch deserves to rot in prison."

"Couldn't agree more. Anyway, I'd better let you get on. Don't go overdoing it. We'll catch up soon. I can't believe you'll be living around the corner from me in a couple of weeks."

"Hardly around the corner, but I get what you mean. Twenty minutes away is better than what it is now. Give my love to Simon. Tell him Tony and I can't wait to see him again."

"I will, love. Promise me you'll take care of yourself at work, take a break if you need to. And when you walk out of the door for the last time, smack DCI Roberts in the mouth for me."

"You're crazy, but I love ya. See you soon, Sally."

CHAPTER 8

Her nerves jangled. If it wasn't her father shouting at her every second of the day, it was Kathryn bending her ear about how dangerous her agenda was turning out to be. She'd had enough. Her head was full of plans that were slowly driving her crazy. She feared either her father or her sister was about to take the brunt of her frustrations.

"I'm scared. Why can't we just take off? Leave this dump?" Kathryn curled up into a ball beside her and trembled.

Claire pulled the blanket over her. "We will, in time. We don't have enough yet. The money we've got stashed away would only see us through a short time. Bear with me, sweetie."

"I'm trying. It's hard. I keep wondering what I'd do without you. If you went to prison for killing…you know. I couldn't go on, not without you by my side. I'm weak, unable to fight for my rights. You're the strongest woman I know, Claire."

"I'll let you into a secret…if anything ever happened to you, I'd crumble in a heartbeat. You're my inspiration. The reason I do what I do. Yes, I protect you, I always have, but it works both ways. If there's no you then there's no me. What's that saying? There's no I in team. That's what we are, love, a *team*. A kick-arse one at that."

They snuggled down together. Soon after Kathryn fell asleep, it wasn't long before she twitched as her nightmares took over, her legs kicking out at Claire. She knew there was no point waking her. It was the same routine every night. Once Kathryn fell into a deeper sleep, that was when she relaxed and the anxious movements ceased. Claire remained awake for another couple of hours, reliving the ordeals of not only the murders she'd recently committed but also the sequence of events the men had forced upon her and her sister at such a young age. She was justified in her actions, there was no doubting that, not in her eyes. Maybe others would have a problem dealing with the situation, though.

Denis's face drifted into her head. In her mind's eye she was ten again. Her father had forced her into the room alone to be with the vile man. He'd stripped her naked and leered at every inch of her pre-adolescent body. She'd trembled, not because the room was cold—no, under his intensive gaze, trying to block out the hatred coursing through her veins. She was aware by now of what to expect. She'd gone through this same ritual more times than she cared to remember. At least twenty times. She'd stopped counting after that.

"Hello, my little China Doll. Come, sit on the bed with me."

She detested the nickname he'd given her after the first time he'd laid his grubby hands on her skin. She'd tried to zone out, the way she always did when she was with him. Most of the time she'd instinctively known what these men wanted. Her father had forced her to watch porn films from the age of six, preparing her for how she should respond to these vile creatures. Denis's hands had slid across her young body, and his lips touched her neck. She'd closed her eyes, trying to block out the emotion building within and striving even harder to suppress the urge to projectile vomit over him.

A cold sweat broke out, covering her flesh. She couldn't think about it any more. It didn't matter now; the man had raped her for the last time. So had Larry. He'd been even worse than Denis in his demands. Over time, he'd become far more brazen in his requests. Degrading images swam in her head. Would she ever be rid of them? The images were burned into her mind. Maybe in time she would, but she feared that day would come only when she'd successfully killed every man on her list. She said each of their names at night, and as her eyes closed, she imagined their screams when she took her revenge.

She drifted off to sleep eventually and woke at nine-thirty the next morning to hear Kathryn crying. Claire sat up and pulled on her sister's shoulder, forcing her to face her. "Hey, what's wrong, love?"

"I'm scared. I had a nightmare. In it the police carted you off. Took you away from me. Don't let them do that, please, Claire. Let's drop all those plans you've made. Take what you have and go."

"We can't, not yet. We've discussed this at length. We simply don't have enough money, not yet, and even—"

Her father's roar interrupted their conversation. Both girls froze and stared at the door. His feet thundered up the stairs, and within seconds he was standing in the doorway of their bedroom, his face almost purple with rage.

"Is something wrong, Father?" Claire asked cautiously.

"Yes. Why are you still in bed? It's nearly ten o'clock. I want to be on the road by eleven."

"Are you going somewhere?"

"We all are. Now get ready. You," he said, pointing at Claire, never one to feel comfortable about using his daughters' names. "Pack my bag as well as your own. Come on, get cracking."

"How long are we going for, Father?" She hated the weakness prevalent in her voice, but it was a necessary evil for her to portray that weakness. He needed to recognise how weak she was to divert any suspicions he may get. Although he was fully aware of what she was capable of, having witnessed her first murder, he had no idea of her recent murderous actions. If he found out, he'd be furious and beat the living shit out of her.

"A few days. Look at it as a kind deed. I'm taking you on holiday to the Lakes. Now get a move on."

He stormed out of the room and back down the stairs.

Claire threw the bedding back. "Come on, we don't have much time. Are you all right to pack your own bag?"

"Of course I am. I'm not a child, you know."

"I know. I'm sorry. Let's get on with it. Make sure you pack some jumpers; the nights can be cold up there."

Kathryn saluted her. "I will, Captain."

Claire ran into the bathroom and stood under the shower for a few minutes, mentally working out what to pack for herself and her father and wondering if they had enough cases for the three of them. She didn't think so. It didn't matter, she could fling her stuff in a black bag. A slight thrill tickled her spine. He'd never taken them on holiday before, which begged the question, why now? Did he know about Denis and Larry?

Kathryn had found a small overnight bag in her wardrobe and was adding the final jumper to it as Claire entered the room. "All set, are you?"

"I think so, do you want to check I haven't forgotten anything?"

"No, I trust you. I think I have a black sack in here." She got down on her hands and knees and rummaged at the bottom of the wardrobe. "Yes." Then she proceeded to bundle as many clothes as she could fit into the bag, aware that her sister would probably borrow some of hers when they got there. Five minutes later, she went into her father's room and hunted in his wardrobe for an old Adidas sports bag he'd picked up from a jumble sale years earlier. She threw a few underwear garments, shirts, trousers and jumpers into it and collected his toiletries from the bathroom.

"Ten minutes. Are you girls ready yet?"

"Soon, Father."

"Get a move on," he yelled angrily. "We leave at eleven on the dot, whether you're ready or not. I don't want to get caught up in the traffic on the M1 and M6."

"I hear you, Father. We're almost there." She flew back into the bedroom she shared with her sister. "All set? Do you have your toiletries?"

"Crap, I knew I'd forget something. What about towels?"

"We'd better take a couple. Can you grab three from the airing cupboard on your way back and throw them in my sack?"

Claire took the other bags downstairs. In the end, they were ready to set off at five minutes to eleven. The only thing left to pack were their shoes. She decided they should all wear their trainers for the journey and take another pair of shoes with them in case their father did something out of character and took them out for a meal during their stay.

Her father inspected their belongings and threw them in the boot of the car. He handed Claire the keys. "You're driving."

Keeping up the pretence, she feigned shock. "I can't. It's been ages since I've driven a car, Father."

"Time you got back in the saddle then, isn't it?" he sneered. Grabbing her painfully around her wrist, he dug the pointed end of one of the keys into the palm of her hand.

Aware of what would happen if she cried out in pain, she remained silent. Instead, she took the keys and nodded at her father.

They set off. Claire intentionally made the first few miles uncomfortable for all of them, pretending that she was feeling strange behind the wheel.

"Get a grip. Sort those gears out, girl. I hope we don't have to contend with this shit all the way up north!"

"It's been a few years since I've driven, Father. Maybe you should drive."

He reached over, his seat belt restraining his movements, and slapped her across the face. "Stop your complaining or I'll give you something to complain about. You hear me?"

"Yes, Father. I'm sorry. It won't happen again."

In the background, Kathryn's stomach rumbled. Neither of them had eaten since six the previous evening. Her own stomach joined in soon after. Her father ignored the noise. Claire knew he would have eaten first thing; he was a creature of habit in that respect. Feeding his own belly while he starved theirs. It was more than she dare do to suggest they stop on the five-hour-plus journey for sustenance. She would only end up getting another backhander.

The traffic on the M6 ground to a halt in one section due to roadworks. This infuriated her father. She flinched several times when he hit the dashboard with his clenched fist.

After that nightmare part of the journey was over, he reluctantly gave in and ordered Claire to pull into the next available services. She smiled at her sister in the rear-view mirror. Kathryn stared back at her, her eyes filled with tears. Claire's heart hurt at the torture her sister was going through. Having food in your belly was a basic necessity in this life, which both of them frequently missed out on. It was obvious that when they returned to the house Claire would need to up the ante. She ran through the list in her mind and picked out a name she knew would lead them to their way out.

"Here. Pull in here, you dozy mare."

Distracted by their plight, she'd almost missed the turning for the services. She found a space close to the entrance. Her father ordered them to stay in the car. Watching him walk towards the huge building, Claire was tempted to take off, but she soon realised how foolish that would be. She needed time to gather her thoughts, to piece things together. She hadn't had time to retrieve any of the money from the attic anyway.

"I can't cope with this. I've had enough," Kathryn complained.

Claire unclipped her seat belt and swivelled in her seat to face her sister. "We have to. Hang in there, sweetie. It's too soon to think about taking off."

"Too soon? We've lived this miserable life for years now. When will it bloody end? I'm constantly ill, I'm undernourished. We both are." She glanced out of the side window and pointed at a young man sitting in a car a few spaces away from them stuffing his face. "What I wouldn't give for a tiny bite of his burger. Look at him. I'm salivating just watching him. It's torture, pure and simple. Why does Father keep us with him, apart from the obvious, that is?"

"To give us our freedom would mean he's failed in this life. I hear you on the food front, I could eat a rotting horse I'm that hungry. Oh crap, he's coming back." Claire swiftly buckled herself in again and started the engine.

Her father flung the door open and dropped into the passenger seat.

Out of her peripheral vision, she noticed three chocolate bars in his hand. Her mouth watered, and she imagined taking a satisfying bite out of each bar.

"Well, what are you waiting for? Drive off."

Her gaze caught her sister's in the mirror. Kathryn shook her head, and a stray tear slid down her cheek. *When will this end? I'll have to think long and hard about that. I'm tempted to end it while we're away. Let's see where we end up first, and then I'll decide.*

Her father fiddled with the satnav, punching in the postcode that would take them to their final destination. He replaced the equipment on its mount on the dashboard and promptly fell asleep with the chocolate bars acting as forms of the most despicable torture ever.

Claire's blood boiled, not for herself, but for Kathryn. Observing her sister in the mirror, she seemed broken almost beyond repair.

The journey was conducted in silence apart from the odd snore which erupted from their father. Kathryn got Claire's attention when she gestured that she wanted to throttle their father while he slept. Claire had to admit the same thought had occurred to her once or twice, too. Claire's mind drifted, back in time to another occasion involving not only Denis but Larry as well. It was her first time with two men in the same room. One depraved individual watching on while the other raped her. She remembered it well. It had been her tenth birthday. Her father had held a 'special' party for her where only *his* friends were invited. That was the year she'd stopped looking forward to celebrating her birthday. He'd ordered each of the men, five in total, to give her a 'special present' she wasn't likely to forget. After enduring two painful hours in the company of the men, she'd bid them farewell and rushed upstairs to her bedroom and flung herself on the bed.

Kathryn was five then. Her sister was annoyed with her, thought she'd missed out on the party. Seeing Claire break down when she'd thrown herself on the bed in tears appeared to soften her heart. Kathryn had stroked Claire's head, telling her over and over that everything would be all right. She'd told her that if Father had upset her on her birthday, she was sure he hadn't meant to do it.

Claire smiled up at her, looking into the eyes of a child whose innocence would be stripped from her in years to come. How she'd hated her father that day and every day since. But she hated the men who'd raped her even more.

Her father emitted a loud snore and woke up. "Are we there yet?"

"Not yet. Another hour or so according to the satnav."

He tore open a Mars bar and bit into it, moaning satisfactorily as the chocolate combined with the toffee and soft nougat in his mouth. Kathryn's tummy rumbled once more as envy struck. Neither of them spoke. They sat there in silence as their father proceeded to pile on the torture. Claire clenched her fists tighter around the steering wheel, forcing back the temper rising within.

Finally, after he'd completed his chocolate bar, he threw one over his shoulder to Kathryn. She ripped the wrapper off and gobbled three consecutive mouthfuls without taking a breath.

"Take your time," Claire ordered her sister.

"Leave her alone to enjoy it. You're always bossing her around. Don't think it goes unnoticed, bitch."

"I do no such thing," she snapped back.

His fist hit the side of her face. The car swerved and the vehicle behind blasted its horn.

"Shut the fuck up. Stop arguing with me. That's it, I'm going to have your bar now."

Claire stared in the mirror. Kathryn quickly shoved the rest of her Mars in her mouth. Their gazes locked; there was no remorsefulness in her sister's eyes. Her survival instinct had kicked in, that much was evident.

Claire's stomach rumbled for the rest of the journey. She slowed and approached the log cabin on the banks of a large lake. She didn't have a clue where they were. The three of them unloaded the car—well, Kathryn and Claire did most of the work, her father keen on dishing out the instructions as usual. It wasn't until they rounded the corner that Claire spotted another cabin around twenty feet away from them. She exhaled a relieved breath. Maybe they wouldn't be alone up here after all. Her father was usually on his best behaviour when they weren't alone. She had a spring in her step now and gathered the rest of their belongings to take to the cabin. She paused and stared across the lawn between them and the other cabin as a horrible thought descended. *Maybe the cabin would be empty during our stay.* She said a little prayer, hoping she was wrong.

Once all the bags were transferred into the cabin and the girls had unpacked their belongings, Claire figured out how to boil the kettle, and with her father's permission, made them all a coffee. The inside of her mouth tasted like coarse sandpaper. It had been almost twenty-four hours since the last cup of coffee had passed her lips.

Every now and again, she snuck a look out of the window at the cabin next door, eager to see if any residents arrived. But her father caught her and slapped her around the face and ordered her to sit down. The three of them sat there in silence. There was no food in the cupboards, and her father hadn't instructed her to stop off at the supermarket en route. What, and when, would they eat?

She sat on the fabric sofa and rested her elbow on the wooden arm, Kathryn alongside her, her stomach rumbling louder than ever.

"Can't you shut that thing up?" her father demanded, leaping out of his chair and pacing the floor in front of them.

"I can't. I'm hungry. We both are," Kathryn mumbled. She sank back in her chair out of reach. But it wasn't long before the palm of his hand connected with her cheek.

Claire jumped to her feet and stood between her father and her sister. "Don't lay another hand on her."

"It's all right, Claire, he didn't hurt me."

Her father closed the gap between them. His face lowered to within inches of her own. She smelt his nicotine breath and wanted to retch.

"You don't want to do this, girl. Sit down and shut up."

"I do. We need food. You ate in the car and probably had breakfast before we set off. Our last meal was at six last night."

Outside, a car rumbled past the cabin and stopped.

"That's our food delivery now. What? Did you think I had forgotten?" he challenged her. Her father marched towards the door, yanked it open and stepped outside. "Great timing. How was your trip?"

Claire sat next to her sister. They clutched hands and stared at the open doorway. She strained an ear, trying to figure out who her father was having a conversation with. It was impossible to make out what the new arrival was saying.

"Come in when you want. I'll get the plates ready."

"I'll eat mine out of the wrapper," one of the newcomers yelled.

"That's fine by me, we all will," her father replied. He walked through the doorway and shouted, "Well, don't just sit there. Get the kettle on for our guests, they've brought food." He looked down at the carrier bag in his hand which was bulging with a takeaway.

Her stomach rumbled loudly as the smell invaded her nostrils. *I hope some of that food is for us and not another one of his twisted games.* She'd known that to happen over the years. Her father liked nothing more than to try out that particular torture method now and again.

Claire and Kathryn left their seats. Claire filled the kettle and asked Kathryn to get the knives and forks from the drawer in the kitchenette. Footsteps approached on the decked area out front, and Claire's gaze flew to the door. Standing in the doorway were two men on her list. The realisation of why they were there quickly followed.

Her father was about to pimp them out again.

CHAPTER 9

Lorne and the team had their usual meeting first thing in the morning, and it was decided that with very little for them to go on they would make use of the notebook. The team had worked hard to gather the information they needed about the men, such as their addresses and their roles in the community, and only their background checks were incomplete at this point. However, Lorne was keen to press on, and now she and Katy were on their way to the first person on that list. A Wayne Jethrum. They arrived at the mid-terraced house and were welcomed by a woman in her late forties. Sandra Jethrum took them on an unexpected tour of the downstairs, proud of the recent renovations she and her husband had carried out.

"It's wonderful. Must have cost you a fortune? Sorry, that was nosy of me. I didn't mean anything by that comment; I used to renovate houses myself."

"Ah, that explains the compliment then. So pleased you like it. It's silly of me I know, but I find myself walking on air around here now. You should have seen it before. It was a mouldy excuse for a house. We moved in six months ago and paid for an architect to redesign the downstairs for us because it simply wasn't working. We're delighted with the results."

"Isn't it amazing what an architect can do with a place?" Lorne said, admiring the detail of the interior, her envy gene twitching a little.

"It is. We've never considered going down that route before, but it was worth the expense. Okay, now I've done all my showing off, perhaps you wouldn't mind telling me what brings two policewomen to my door?" Sandra motioned for them to sit at the large kitchen table in the open-plan kitchen-diner at the rear of the property. It overlooked a small terraced garden that Lorne assumed had been landscaped as part of the renovations.

"We were hoping to have a brief chat with your husband. I'm presuming he's at work?"

"Not today, he's not. He's gone up to the Lakes for a few days with a couple of his pals. They take off on a fishing expedition now and again, when one of them is feeling stressed. Not that I mind. You know how it is, ladies, we girls prefer to have the house to ourselves at times, right?"

Lorne smiled and nodded, even though she couldn't imagine being at home without Tony, not now he was retired from MI6. She loved having him around, getting under her feet. "How long have they gone for?"

"Three days. It's a shorter trip than usual. Don, that's his best mate, well, he rang a day or two back and asked how Wayne was fixed. Never one to shirk his duties at the shop, my husband arranged cover and agreed to go within ten minutes flat. Shame he doesn't give me the same consideration when I suggest going away. Men, eh? They're a law unto themselves at times. Still, he's a lovely man, not sure what I'd do without him."

"Have you been together long?"

"Twenty-two years."

"Do you have any children?" Her observations of the spick and span area suggested not.

"Sadly, no. I was unable to carry a baby full term. After having four miscarriages, I decided to stop trying. I couldn't put myself through the trauma any more. Wayne reluctantly agreed with me. He was desperate to have kids, but we're over that now. We have skirted around possibly adopting a child in the near future. I think our ages will go against us on that one. Sorry, you don't want to hear the ins and outs of our daily lives."

"I'm sorry you were unable to have children of your own. Maybe you'll get your wish of adopting a child in the near future."

"I doubt it." She held up her crossed fingers. "You never know. We'll keep trying."

"You do that. Everyone should have dreams they wish to fulfil in this life."

"I sincerely believe in that. I have several precious stones et cetera placed around the house, hoping they'll bring me luck."

Lorne could tell that Katy was eager to get on as she spotted her crossing and uncrossing her legs under the table.

"The reason we're here is because we'd like to speak to your husband about a list of names we've found."

Sandra's brow wrinkled, and she tilted her head. "I'm not with you. What list?"

Lorne produced the little notebook still in the evidence bag and placed it on the table.

Sandra's smile dropped, and she stared at the notebook. "I'm not liking the sound of this. Please, spare me any small talk and get to the point, Inspector."

"Very well. It's early days in our investigation so far, but as I said, this notebook has come into our possession."

"How? What investigation?"

"We're investigating the murders of two men."

Sandra gasped and fell back in her chair. "Murder? In this neck of the woods? That's unbelievable."

Not as unbelievable as you're thinking, not in the city of London, dear lady. "Not really, the crime rate is escalating in this area."

"Oh my. Okay, that aside, what has this got to do with my husband? No! You don't suspect him of murdering these two men? That's unthinkable, he'd never do something as terrible as that. Not my Wayne."

Lorne smiled to reassure the woman. "No, we don't believe he's killed anyone. However, we have a list of men here, one of whom is your husband, and two out of the six men have lost their lives in the past few days."

Sandra gasped again and reached for her phone. "I have to ring him. To warn him he could be in danger."

"All we're seeking to do at this stage is try to find out if your husband knew these other men."

"Let me ring him, and you can ask the question. He's driving at the moment but he has hands-free in the car. Let me try."

Lorne nodded. With her hand shaking, Sandra punched in a number and put the phone on speaker. All three of them listened to the phone ring five times before the voicemail message kicked in.

Lorne shook her head. "Don't leave a message."

Sandra sighed and ended the call. "That's strange, he always answers his phone."

"Maybe the phone is in a black spot and unable to connect. Or he could be out of the car at the services getting a drink to break up his journey. Perhaps we could try again in a few minutes."

"Perhaps. Talking of drinks, I could do with a cuppa. What about you, ladies?"

Both Lorne and Katy agreed and asked for a coffee.

With the drinks made, Sandra placed another call to her husband. This time the phone rang twice and then was answered, "Hi, love. What's up? I can't talk for long, and the reception will probably be a bit dodgy as we're surrounded by hills."

"Wayne, I have two police officers with me. They're investigating the murders of two men. Hang on, it's complicated, I'll hand you over to the officer in charge."

"Hello, Mr Jethrum, this is DI Lorne Warner. I'm dealing with the investigation into the deaths of a Denis Tallon and a Larry Small. Do you know these men?"

There was silence on the other end of the line. The only thing that Lorne could make out was the noise of the traffic on a busy stretch of the motorway. "Wayne, can you hear me?"

"Sorry, bit distracted there as we're coming up to the slip road we're looking for. Yes, I know of both men. I can't believe what you're telling me. Dead? They're both dead? Was it an accident? No, Sandra mentioned they were both murdered," he said, asking and answering his own question.

"That's right. We can't go into details but we're interested to speak to you and a few other men, the names of which we found in a book at Larry's address. How did you know these men, sir?"

"Umm...they're old acquaintances of mine. I haven't seen either of them for around ten years—no, more than that, maybe fifteen years."

"How were you connected? By that I mean, why were you friends back then but haven't seen each other in all that time?"

"Gosh, I can't remember. What is this? Are you accusing me of bumping these guys off?"

"No, sir, not in the slightest. We're simply trying to piece the puzzle together. How did you know them?"

Again, there was a strained silence for a few seconds. "Er...we belonged to a bridge club."

Lorne's gut told her he was lying. "What was the name of the club where you played bridge, sir?"

"Shit! I don't know. Listen, lady, I'm busy. You know how dangerous it is to hold a conversation and drive at the same time."

"I appreciate that, sir. Maybe you could ring me the moment you get to your destination. It really is urgent."

"What? Why? I can't add anything to what I've already told you."

"Please, sir."

"Okay. You need to tell me how my friends were murdered first?"

"I can't give out those details over the phone, I'm sorry."

The call was disconnected.

"I'll try and ring him back." Sandra tried, and the phone rang and rang until the voicemail message came on.

"Don't worry. When is your husband due back?"

"On Friday, not until the evening, though. Will you pop back and see him then?"

"Yes, we'd much prefer to see people in person wherever possible."

"I understand. I'm sorry I can't help you at all. I know my husband had a group of friends he hung out with at the time he suggested, but I'm afraid I didn't know their names. I've learnt something new tonight."

"Oh, what's that?"

"That my husband plays bridge. Who'd have thought that? Not me, that's for sure."

Lorne and Katy finished their drinks and stood to leave. Lorne said, "We'll return on Friday. Thanks for your hospitality, Mrs Jethrum."

"I'll show you to the door. Sorry we couldn't be of more help." She smiled and closed the front door behind them.

"Well, that was convenient."

Lorne frowned and looked over the roof of the car. "What was?"

Katy got in the passenger seat beside her. "His phone cutting out like that during his trip."

"Yep, it hadn't gone unnoticed. I wonder if he's really going on a fishing trip or if he has something else in mind."

"I guess we won't find that out until Friday when he comes back." Katy shuddered. "I hope he's not up to his old tricks, if indeed he is part of this suspected paedophile ring."

"Yep, I was thinking along the same lines. Okay, let's set Jethrum aside for now and move on to the next name on the list. Can you enter the address into the satnav for me?"

Katy fished a sheet of A4 paper out of her pocket and punched in the details. "Isaac Frost, his house is a few streets away from here."

Lorne turned the engine over and drove off. Within ten minutes, they parked up outside another mid-terraced house. This time the property was in dire need of repair. Chipped paint was visible on the windowsills, and the front patch of garden was overgrown and sprouting weeds everywhere. "It's like chalk and cheese."

"Yep, the Jethrums' house had a superb kerb appeal. This one looks shit."

Lorne giggled. "Get you, with your fancy terms. 'Kerb appeal.'"

Katy yanked on the handle and left the car. "Kerb appeal isn't fancy."

"I know. I'm winding you up. Never thought I'd see the day those words tumbled out of your mouth. Let's hope we get more joy from this stop."

Lorne used the sleeve of her jacket to ring the grimy doorbell. Katy sniggered at her prudish behaviour.

"Hey, have you seen the state of it? You have no idea what kind of germs fester on doorbells. I read an article in a magazine only last week."

"Give us a break, Lorne." Katy tutted.

"Okay." She grinned sheepishly. They waited several minutes after which Lorne rang the bell a few times more. "I don't think anyone is in. Let's see if the neighbour knows anything."

They left the withered and dying garden and ventured up the path of the immaculately cared-for garden next door.

"Crap, I bet these guys are furious with Frost for not keeping his front up to scratch. Makes you wonder what the rear garden is like," Lorne whispered.

"I bet it's rat infested," Katy mumbled.

Lorne rang the bell. This time she didn't bother using the cuff of her jacket to touch the button.

A lady in her sixties appeared soon after. She had a yapping Jack Russell in her arm. "Hello," she screeched over the racket. "Polly, quiet with you now."

The dog instantly stopped barking and growled instead when Lorne produced her ID. "Hello, there. I'm Detective Inspector Lorne Warner, and this is Detective Sergeant Katy Foster. Sorry to disturb you."

"Oh, the police. Whatever has happened? Oh my, it's not my sister, is it? We lost touch a few years ago after a silly argument. I knew I should have got in touch with her. Neither of us are getting any younger."

"No, it's not concerning your sister. It's nothing to worry about, a general enquiry really. We were hoping you could possibly tell us about your neighbour." Lorne pointed in the direction of Frost's house.

"Ah, well, that's a relief. Gosh, my heart almost stopped pumping for a second there. Right, what do you want to know? Do you want to come in?"

"If you wouldn't mind, the wind is a bit nippy today."

"Come on in. I'll pop Polly in her basket in the lounge. Won't be a tick, dears."

They waited in the hallway for the old lady to re-join them.

"Right, what is it you want to know about them?"

"Them? I take it there's a Mrs Frost?"

"I don't know about that. If there ever was one, I think she left years ago. Isaac lives there with his two daughters."

"I see. How old are the daughters?"

"Now you're testing me. Maybe twenty-five and twenty-one—don't quote me on that, though. When you get to my time of life, you have no concept of youngsters' ages."

"That's okay. Do you know either of the girls' names?"

"The older one is Claire. Not sure on the younger one as I rarely see her. Don't see much of either of them really. I hear them more than I see them."

"As in they play loud music?" Lorne enquired, her interest spiking up a notch.

"No, nothing like that. He tends to shout a lot at the girls. At first, I thought he had a hearing problem. I mentioned it to another neighbour, and they told me to get used to it, that he's always shouting at the poor girls. I wished I'd heard them when I came to view the damn house. They say you should check out a property at different hours of the day to see what the noise level is like, don't they?"

"That's a shame. Have you lived here long, Mrs...sorry, I didn't catch your name?"

"Lewis, Gladys Lewis. Around four years, give or take a few months. As you can see, I look after my house and garden. There are three adults living there, and look at the state of the place. I wouldn't be able to sell my house even if I tried, so I don't bother. It would be more hassle than it's worth. No, when he starts yelling, I turn the TV up nice and loud. He tends to bang on the wall then, shouting expletives at me, but I don't care. We're all entitled to live peacefully in our own homes, aren't we? Or is that too much to ask now? Only we have a couple of those boy racers living around here, their souped-up cars making a right racket at all hours of the day and night. What is wrong with people? That's the trouble, there's no damn respect nowadays. God, I sound like my bloody mother, I know, but it's the damn truth. Oops, there I go again. You don't want to hear about my problems."

"That's okay, Mrs Lewis. Maybe if you reported your grievances to the council, they might help you a little."

"Been there, done that, and got absolutely zilch in return. As long as it doesn't affect the people at the council, they couldn't care bloody less about my sanity or needs for living a peaceful existence."

"Maybe I can place a call for you when we return to the station."

Her eyes widened. "Would you? That would be amazing if you would."

"I'll try. Anyway, we've knocked next door and couldn't get an answer. Have you seen the family at all lately?"

"I was putting something in my bin earlier and saw all three of them getting in the father's car. Hang on a second, yes, they were each holding a bag of sorts. One of those sports bags and a few black sacks."

"They've gone away then. It's a long shot, but I don't suppose you'd know where or for how long?"

"No. I was surprised to see them getting in the car. I never speak to them, dear, so I'm sorry, I can't tell you more."

"Not to worry. Do you think any of the other neighbours would know?"

She shook her head. "Sadly not. I speak to the others regularly. We've got a nice little community going on here, and they refuse to be a part of it. Always shouting out of the window that we're nosy *feckers*, I think is the word he prefers to use. Rude man, one of the rudest I've ever had the displeasure of laying my eyes on."

"Thanks for being honest with us. Okay, we'll leave you to enjoy your peace while they're away."

"Do you want me to tell them you want to speak to them when they get back? I hate talking to them but I will, if you want me to."

"Perhaps if I leave you a card you wouldn't mind ringing me when they return. That would be a great help."

"Of course. I like to help the police out where I can. This country of ours needs sorting out. I know you officers are under a terrible strain with your resources. It shows, doesn't it? With the crime rate going up yearly. My father used to walk the beat back in the sixties. It was a whole different kettle of fish back then." She laughed.

"I bet," Lorne replied, laughing with the woman.

"He worked the beat near our home. The number of times I saw him march a brat of a kid by the scruff of his neck past our front window is nobody's business. Those were the days, I can tell you. He took pride in his role in the community; everyone looked up to my old Dad. He was commended for breaking up a hard gang at one time. He heard a whisper on the street from one of his contacts and set the wheels in motion to arrest the gang. If it hadn't been for Dad's hard work, we would be reading about another huge robbery in our history books...you know, like the Brink's-Mat one."

"That's wonderful to hear. You must be so proud of him. It's not often we hear of such bravery by officers these days. Policing has certainly changed over the years."

"And not for the better, I can hear my father saying now." She rolled her eyes and crossed her arms.

"That's true. Anyway, I could stand here all day discussing the ins and outs of what's wrong with our society today, but the truth is, we have work to do on a very important case. Thank you for your time. I'll look forward to hearing from you when the family returns, whenever that may be."

"As soon as they step out of the car, I'll call you."

"Thank you. Speak soon, Mrs Lewis."

"Good luck, ladies. I know it's probably rude of me to ask why you want to speak to the family, but I'm going to chance my arm anyway."

"We're investigating a couple of crimes, and Mr Frost's name has cropped up during our enquiries. It's nothing to worry about, we only wanted a brief chat with him."

"Gosh, that's all right then. As long as I don't have a serial killer living next door, I'll be able to sleep at night now."

"No fear of that." Lorne opened the front door, and she and Katy left the house. She waved at the old lady from the gate before getting in the car.

"Nice old dear," Katy said, buckling herself in.

"Yep, she seems it. Interesting what she said about the father always shouting at the girls. Strange they're both still at home at that age, don't you think?"

"Not really. It's getting increasingly difficult for youngsters to get on the property ladder these days, or hadn't you heard about that?"

Lorne pulled a face at her partner. "I see your sarcastic gene is rearing its head again, Katy."

"Sorry. I didn't mean to snap. I'm frustrated about the case. I feel like we're being given the runaround."

"Everything will drop into place eventually, I promise you. Right, let's head for the next one on our list, see if we get any luck there."

Katy punched in the postcode for the following location and sat back. A subdued atmosphere filled the car until Katy announced, "I'm just throwing this out there... What if there's something in the fact that Wayne Jethrum and the Frost family are both away at the moment?"

"You mean they've contacted each other and took off because of that list being discovered?"

"I don't know. All I'm saying is that it's not the holiday season yet; however, the people we're keen to speak with have all taken off at the same time."

"Hmm...you have a genuine point there. You know how much I hate working with coincidences. That's a pretty major one you've highlighted."

"Why don't we hold off doing anything for now and see what happens at the next address?"

"Agreed. It's definitely an interesting scenario you've raised."

Within fifteen minutes, they arrived at the home of another person of interest on their list. This time the house was a bungalow on a quiet cul-de-sac just north of town.

"Now this appears to be a far nicer area. Haven't been around these parts before," Lorne said.

"It's all right, if you like bungalows. They're for old people, so I tend to steer clear of them. Not that I'm looking to move anytime soon. Oh heck, I'm talking a lot of crap, ignore me."

Lorne giggled. "I thought Mrs Lewis had swapped places with you then."

Katy huffed, unhooked her seat belt and stepped out of the vehicle. "Bloody charming, that is," she fired over the roof of the car when Lorne emerged.

"It was a joke, Katy. Lighten up."

"Sorry. I'm wound up. We've been out here most of the morning, for what? Diddly squat, that's what."

"Don't lose faith. You know how it is with these types of cases. The general public expect clues to drop into our laps. The reality is that things never turn out that way. Stay with the programme, love."

"I will. It doesn't prevent me from wanting to vent, Lorne."

"Do you want to take the lead on this one, is that it? You're feeling left out of it?"

"Not at all. I'm easy either way. I just want to get back to real policing, not chasing people who are trying to avoid us."

Lorne sighed. "We don't have proof of that, not yet, Katy."

"Okay, if you say so. I'm thinking we have a list of men, two of whom are now lying in the mortuary fridge, and two men who have suddenly felt the need to take off, probably after hearing about the deaths of their friends."

"Or it could all be a huge coincidence."

Katy cocked an eyebrow as Lorne rang the bell to the bungalow. She bent over and sniffed an early flowering rose planted up a trellis right by the front door. The sweet smell had an instant effect on her. It brightened her mood considerably.

"Sniff that. That'll ease the tension coursing through your veins."

"Don't be so ridiculous," Katy admonished.

The front door opened to reveal a blonde woman with purple highlights in her hair. She wore a leopardskin jumpsuit and high heels as if she was about to go out somewhere. "Yes? If you're selling something, I'm not interested. So bugger off."

Lorne produced her ID and held it up in the woman's heavily made-up face. "We're not. Mrs Barton, I presume?"

"What if I am? What do you want?"

"A quick chat with your husband if you don't mind. Is he at home by any chance?"

"What about?"

"Would you mind if we discussed this inside, Mrs Barton?"

She removed her hand from the door, crossed her arms and tapped her foot. "You're not stepping foot inside this house, not without a warrant. Have you got one of those?"

"No. Do you think we need one? You're giving us the impression that you're keen to hide something. What would that be, Mrs Barton?"

"I'm not. That's your sodding suspicious mind swinging into action, take my word on that. I don't let coppers in my house, full stop. My brother was stitched up good and proper by your mob a few years back. Say what you've got to say, and let me get on with what I was doing."

"And what was that, Mrs Barton?"

"None of your damned business. What do you want with my husband?"

"All will be revealed in good time. Is he here?"

"No," she replied, her lips thinning in anger.

"Is he at work?" Lorne asked through gritted teeth. This woman was doing a good job of rubbing her up the wrong way. If she wasn't careful, Lorne would arrest her for obstructing an investigation.

"No."

"Okay, we're clearly not getting very far here. Get your coat, Mrs Barton, we'll conduct this interview down at the station."

"What frigging interview? You said you wanted a chat with my husband. I told you he wasn't here. I'm not going anywhere with the likes of you."

"Look, you've already told me your brother had problems with the police. I'm not aware of the incident, but being obstructive with us isn't helping either your husband or yourself, is it?"

"Say what you like, I ain't going nowhere with you. Wait here. I'm going to ring my solicitor. He'll tell you where to get off harassing me, lady."

"It's inspector, and I've done nothing of the sort. We're investigating two major crimes in the area, and all I'd like to do is have a chat with your husband. Now, where is he?" Lorne demanded, her temper matching the obstinate woman's.

"Away."

"Away where?"

"Why? You have no right to pry into our personal life. I don't have a problem with my husband going away, why should you?"

"Just answer the damn question," Katy pressed, surprising Lorne.

The woman glared at both of them and then exhaled a large breath. "He's gone fishing with a mate. Is there a law against that?"

"No, not at all. Who has he gone away with?" Lorne asked, even though the reply was going to be an obvious one.

"A mate of his called Wayne Jethrum. They quite often take off for a few days."

"To the Lakes?"

Mrs Barton frowned. "Yes, how do you know that?"

"We've just come from Mr Jethrum's house, and his wife told us the same."

"If that's the case, why bother coming here?"

"We have to follow up on the facts. It's never good to take someone's word on things in our line of business."

"Roughly translated that means you don't trust people, right?"

"Not necessarily. We've had instances in the past when a husband has told his wife one thing and done something completely different."

"Ah, like shagging another bird, is that what you're trying to say?"

"On occasion, yes, that's been the outcome. How often does your husband go off with his friend?"

She shrugged. "I don't know, a few times a year. He works hard. It's good for him to get away for a while. I don't have any objections. It gives me the freedom to have fun with my friends. Which reminds me, I have a lunch date, so if you'll excuse me."

"Thanks for the information. One last question. Can you give me the address of where your husband is staying and tell me when he's likely to return?"

"No, I don't have an address. He has his phone with him. Yes, the reception can be a bit dodgy at times, but not all the time. If I need to contact him, I can do it via the phone. He's due back on Friday evening. Is that it?" Her hand latched on to the door again.

"Yes, that's it. Thank you for your assistance."

The door slammed shut in their faces before Lorne could say anything else. "Rude fecking bitch," Lorne complained, swivelling on her heel and marching back to the car.

"It's as if she had something to hide. She's staring at us from the front window."

"Christ!" Lorne held her thumb and forefinger up an inch apart. "I'm this close to going back in there and arresting the bitch."

"For what?"

Lorne growled. "I'm sure I could come up with something. What about wearing an endangered species? Did you see that bloody outfit?"

Katy tilted her head back and roared. "I've heard it all now. You're a scream without meaning to be at times. I'm going to miss you, woman."

They got back in the car. "Thanks, I'm going to miss you, too, Katy. I never thought I'd hear myself say that, especially after working the first few months with you. You were so far up your own backside in those days."

"I know. You've moulded me nicely—that's what's coming next, right?"

Lorne chuckled. "You know me so well. Let's pick up some lunch for the gang and return to base."

"What about this mob? What are we going to do about them?"

"I'm thinking about that one. Any idea how many rental properties there are up in the Lake District?"

Katy puffed out her cheeks. "I'm guessing thousands. We could get their registration numbers and ask Graham to track their vehicles on the cameras."

"We could. I doubt the cameras will go very far, maybe to the end of the motorway and that's it."

She started the engine, and they both looked back at the house to see Mrs Barton giving them a perfect view of her middle finger.

"Old hag. That's it. I'm definitely going to get Karen to dig into her past."

Lorne stopped off at the baker's and picked up a mixture of popular sandwiches on white and brown bread and a packet of jam doughnuts that she knew would satisfy the troops for the rest of the day.

They washed their lunch down with a much-needed cup of caffeine and went over how their respective mornings had panned out. After lunch, Karen got on with obtaining the background checks on each of the men and their families, and Graham got to work on the ANPR side of things. Lorne went into her office and rang Patti to chase up the PMs for both victims.

"Hi, how's it going? Do you have time for a brief chat?" Lorne asked, rubbing at her temple, the first signs of a headache taking root.

"It's going well. I haven't got anything for you as yet. I'm still convinced the crimes were committed by the same person, if that helps?"

"It does and it doesn't. We believe we've stumbled across a paedophile ring, but as yet, we haven't had the chance to speak to any of the men involved. We found a list at the second victim's house. It was well hidden, so we're presuming the list is damning in some way."

"Interesting. You're thinking that one of this gang's victims is now on a revenge mission?"

"Yep, it's the only explanation we can come up with for now. It's still a frustrating one to tackle. The men we're trying to interview all appear to be away on holiday, a fishing trip according to a couple of their wives. The other man we're keen to speak with has gone away with his two daughters."

"On the same trip?" Patti asked, her voice rising a little.

"We're unclear about that. All we can do is make an assumption for now."

"Okay, well, I don't really know what to say about that."

"Yeah, I'm at a loss what to think about it, too. I'm trying not to think the worst but have to say I'm struggling. We're doing background checks on everyone involved. Hopefully something will show up there. If not, well, we're no further forward."

"You sound defeated. Don't let the case get to you, mate. Just think, you've only got seven days before you hang up your handcuffs for good."

"I can't bloody wait either. I'd love to go out with a bang by solving this one. Okay, I'll let you get on. Keep me up to date on things, as and when you can, Patti."

"I will. Keep positive, Lorne."

CHAPTER 10

THE MEN, Wayne and Don, had brought with them fish and chips which they'd picked up a few miles down the road. Everyone was hungry and refused to wait for the oven to warm up, so they dug in to the lukewarm meal.

Claire and Kathryn glanced at each other when they saw there were five bundles, one for each of them. Maybe the men weren't so bad after all. Whenever their father bought fish and chips, he only ever forked out for one portion between the three of them, her father having eighty percent of the helping.

They all ate with their fingers. Claire tried to savour every mouthful; however, the hunger pains were driving her nuts, and she ended up wolfing down her meal, finishing long before any of the others with Kathryn doing the same thing and finishing a close second.

Wayne and Don laughed.

"What is it with your girls, Isaac, don't you feed them?" Wayne joked.

Her father glared at his daughters. "Yeah, it's been a long day. Must be all this fresh air that's worked wonders with their appetite, eh, girls?"

Claire wiped the grease from around her mouth on the sleeve of her baggy sweatshirt, which disguised how thin she'd become recently through their father's wilful neglect to allow them any food.

"Okay, now that dinner is out of the way, why don't you guys get unpacked in the cabin next door? I went in there earlier to light the fire, so it should be warm and cosy," her father said, acting like the perfect host.

Wayne and Don attempted to tidy away the remains of their meal, but her father stopped them.

"That's okay, the girls will do it."

The men smiled and walked towards the front door to leave the cabin.

"God, I almost forgot. I received a call on the way up here," Wayne announced.

Her father gestured for him to say more.

"It was the police. They said that Denis and Larry were both dead."

"What?" her father shouted. "How? An accident?"

"Nope, the policewoman told me they'd been murdered."

Claire clutched her sister's hand under the table, urging her not to react to the news as their father's gaze drifted their way. Claire stared down at the table until she sensed him turn away.

"Damn. London is getting worse, isn't it? Bloody knife crimes, I should think. What did you say?"

Wayne shrugged. "Told them I hadn't seen them in years. Then I made out the reception was bad. I have a feeling the woman will contact me again on Friday when I get home. Sad to think we'll never see either of them again."

"Yep. We'll have a drink in their honour over the next few days. You go and get settled," Isaac ordered both men.

As soon as the door closed behind them, their father stood, leaned on the table with one hand and swiped first Claire around the face and then Kathryn. Her sister yelped out in pain. Claire refused to give him the satisfaction of knowing he'd hurt her.

"Show me up eating like that again, and you'll both be sorry. You hear me?"

They both nodded and then flinched when he yelled in their faces.

"I said, do you hear me?"

"Yes, Father," Claire mumbled.

Kathryn followed suit.

"Right, what do you know about Denis and Larry, anything?"

Claire shook her head. "No, Father, it's dreadful news. Sorry about your friends."

"Whatever. Makes no odds to me. Now clear this mess up and then clean yourselves up. You have work to do this evening."

"What work?" Claire asked, the words slipping out before she had a chance to engage her brain.

Her father wiggled his eyebrows, and an evil grin appeared on his ageing face.

Claire shook her head. "No, Father. We won't do it. Not any more, we're grown women. You can't force us to sleep with these men."

"Watch your mouth, bitch. While you're under my roof, you'll do as you're effing well told."

Kathryn gripped Claire's hand tightly. "Please, Father. I don't want to do it, don't make us."

His eyes seemed to change colour, becoming blacker as his gaze intensified. "Let's put it this way: we're a long way from home—either you spread your legs for those two in there or you both walk back to London tomorrow, you got that? Oh, and if you think you've been dealt a poor hand, just think of all the depraved individuals out there who are stalking the motorways, waiting to pounce on innocent girls like you, hitching a bloody ride. Are you getting my drift?"

Kathryn sobbed loudly.

Claire squeezed her hand, imploring her not to show how upset she was, realising what the consequences would be. "Yes, Father. We understand, don't we, Kathryn? Come on, we'll go and get ready."

Her wide-eyed sister looked up and stared at her. Claire tugged at her hand, encouraging her to go with her. Once they were alone in the tiny bedroom, Claire held her sister by the shoulders and shook her slightly.

"Kathryn, you're breaking my heart. We have to do what he says and sleep with these men. Just lie back and think of England. Once we're back in London, I'll punish them all, and we'll take the money and run. Just play along with me on this one for now."

The tears dripped down her sister's cheeks. "I can't do it any more, Claire. I'm tired of being treated like, and living like, a whore. We deserve better than this. When is it all going to end?"

Claire held her close and hugged her tightly. "I know, love. It won't be for long. I have a plan but I need to slot things into position before it can be fulfilled. Are you with me?"

Her sister swallowed hard and nodded.

Claire pushed her gently away from her and wiped Kathryn's eyes with her fingers. "Remember how much I love you. Do as they say, and we'll be okay. If you rebel now, there's no telling what they're likely to do to us up here." As soon as the words left her mouth, she regretted saying them.

"Don't say that, Claire, I'm scared enough as it is. Why do these men do these despicable things to us?"

"If only I could answer that for you. The truth is, I can't. This has nothing to do with us, remember that. We're caught in a vile trap; however, if you're prepared to trust me, then I'll get us out of this mess. I've had enough of being—for want of a better word—a prostitute, lining father's pockets. It's time we stood up for ourselves. We can't do that until we have more funds behind us. Father pulled a fast one on us today by springing this trip on us. All it means is that our departure has been put on hold for a few days. Stay strong, love."

Kathryn stared at her, her eyes dead of all emotion. She hugged her again. They parted swiftly when their father's fist pounded on the door.

"Are you ready yet?"

"Nearly, Father."

"Get a bloody move on."

CLAIRE MADE her father's breakfast of bacon, sausage and fried eggs, which Wayne and Don had brought with them. If it had been up to their father to supply their basic needs, all of them would have starved to death by now. Claire and Kathryn each nibbled on a slice of toast and butter, staring at their father's plate with resentment.

He ate his breakfast with a smug look on his face, letting out a satisfactory moan now and then just to wind them up.

The past two days had been hellish for the girls. Although the men had conversed with them over the dinner table and explained that they'd told their respective wives this was a fishing trip, it turned out to be nothing of the sort.

Claire and Kathryn had been forced to 'service' the men and care for their every need while they, in return, fed them. This was their final day. Her poor sister had complained only an hour before that 'down below' felt like it was on fire. Claire feared her sister had picked up one of those damned infections. If she wasn't angry before about the situation they'd been forced into, she damn well was now. Now she had a new plan festering. London could wait. This new plan couldn't.

"Are you girls packed?"

"Yes, I just have your bag to do. I need to fill the car up with petrol for the journey, too. I'll nip out when the boys leave. Kathryn, will you be a love and pack Father's bag while I'm gone?"

Kathryn nodded, thankfully not giving away anything in her expression in their father's presence.

"Good idea. Once we're on the road, I don't intend stopping," her father said, his mouth full of bacon and sausage.

Claire excused herself from the table and slipped on her shoes and her light jacket.

"Don't be long," he bellowed behind her.

She closed the door and gave him an imaginary finger.

Outside the cabin, she acted shyly in the men's company. "Are you ready to set off?"

"We are. No chance of a quickie this morning, is there?" Wayne joked, placing a finger under her chin, forcing her to look at him.

"Maybe. Not here. I have to nip out for petrol. We could stop down the road for half an hour if you like? No, wait, we'd better not. We have a long trip ahead of us."

"No, I think you're right, a quick one will set us up for the long journey. What do you say, Don? Are you up for it?"

Don rubbed his hands together in glee. "And some. It's just what the doctor ordered, I reckon."

Wayne laughed. "Whatever. We're ready to get on the road now. We'll just say cheerio to your father and Kathryn first."

"I'll wait in the car." She smiled shyly at the two men and raced towards the vehicle.

During her time in the kitchenette that morning, her father had been distracted with an article in the paper the other men had left behind in their cabin. Claire had removed a large knife from the block on the worktop. She stored it in the glove box and started the engine. After turning the car around, she waited for the two men to place their bags in the boot of their vehicle and follow her.

Claire's heart was pounding like an express train, and the adrenaline pumped through her system at what was to come. If a career advisor had told her years ago that she would become a serial killer, she wouldn't have believed them. She hated the thought of giving herself such a tag, especially in the circumstances. She saw herself as more of a 'retribution seeker', fighting for justice for her and her sister after these men had abused them non-stop for years. She hadn't thought about how wrong her actions were because all she cared about was rescuing her sister, giving Kathryn, and herself, for that matter, the life they deserved. One that didn't involve having sex against their wills with often fat, balding men, whom her father had done a deal with.

'Dealing with the Devil', that was how she'd referred to it at one time when speaking about their predicament with Kathryn. She had agreed. Well, the Devil's days were numbered. The pain between her legs from the past few days enforced the feelings of hatred she had for her father. How could he? What man would do that to his own children? All right, he hadn't had sex with them for years himself, he'd become impotent many moons ago, but it hadn't prevented him from pimping them out to his friends.

The men put the last bag in the car and drove past her. She

followed them to the petrol station a couple of miles up the road. While she filled up the car, Wayne came to speak to her. Don was inside, paying for the petrol.

"Did you see that lane up the road?" she asked, a false smile set firmly in place.

"No, I must have missed it. We'll follow you. Can't wait to give you a special farewell gift," he said, reaching down and rubbing the crotch of his trousers.

"What I have planned will be super special, I guarantee it," she teased, shyly looking away from him.

He ran a hand down her cheek. "If only I wasn't married. I'd take you home with me and treat you well. Feed you up for a start, you're too thin."

"That would be wonderful. We can all dream of a better life. I know I would have one with you, Wayne."

"Say the word, and I'd boot Sandra out tomorrow to have you permanently in my bed."

"I couldn't do that to another woman. Maybe if you feel like that you should divorce her. Once a divorce is finalised, things will be better for us."

"I'll think about that, but I don't suppose it will take much thinking about, knowing what the outcome will be."

"Come on, you two. Time's getting on," Don shouted from behind the steering wheel.

"I'm almost done here. Just need to secure the cap and pay, and I'll be with you."

"Can't wait," Wayne whispered, returning to the car.

Claire resisted the temptation to shudder until she was safely inside the shop. She paid for the petrol and then left. At the side of the car was a dispenser. She tore out a couple of plastic gloves and slipped into the driver's seat of her father's car.

She led the men back to the lane she had spotted half a mile up the road. She indicated and turned down the narrow track, praying that it would widen out a bit farther on. Thankfully, it did. The landscape around her was conducive to what she had planned for the two men.

Her mind whirred with what she had in store for them. Wayne would be first, she had decided.

Finding a pull-in along the lane that was big enough for both cars, she indicated. She slipped the gloves on and hid the knife under her jacket, tucking the blade into the top of her trousers, and prayed the blade didn't nick her belly. Then she jumped out of the car, placed her hands in her pockets and shouted for Wayne to join her. There was a small track off to the right that led up a slight incline. Wayne, with his beer belly wobbling, ran to catch up with her.

"Hey," he yelled, struggling to find his breath after only going a few metres. "Wait up! What are we doing up here?"

"I thought it would be more intimate for us up here. You don't want Don watching us, do you? Don't forget, I have something extra special planned for you."

"Okay. I'm all yours. You lead the way, and I'll follow as long as it's not too far."

"Just up here, behind this mound. Trust me." She had spotted the mound from the road and earmarked it for good cover for what she had in mind.

She stood at the top of the hill and glanced back at the two cars. She thanked her lucky stars that Don had remained inside the vehicle. "This is wonderful. The view is spectacular."

Wayne's laboured breath announced his arrival beside her. "It is that." His gaze ran the length of her body. "Now, where's this surprise?"

"Over here. Get your clothes off."

"What? It's far too bloody cold for that."

"Okay, we'd better forget all about it then." She turned in the direction of the cars.

He yanked on her arm. "No, wait. Okay, we'll do this your way. Down here, behind this mound."

She smiled. He'd pointed out the exact position she was thinking of using.

They walked the few feet, and Wayne tore off his clothes. She beamed and pretended she was taking pleasure in his striptease. The truth was, she was trying to force back the bile burning her oesophagus. "Get on your knees." She glanced quickly over her shoulder, ensuring they wouldn't be seen. "Now, tell me why you want to leave your wife. Isn't she good enough for you?"

"What? I don't want to talk about her. All I want is to make love to you."

"Is that what you call it? Making love? I'd call it rape." She whipped out the knife from her jacket and took two steps forward.

He shrank back, beads of sweat profusely breaking out on his forehead. "Claire, I'm sorry. I meant what I said, I want to be with you, if you'll have me?"

"Why would I want a fat bastard like you in my life, shoving his useless cock up me at all hours of the day?" She plunged the knife into his chest and then stood behind him, placed a hand on his forehead and sliced a large gash in his throat.

He gurgled, blood spouted from the wound, and his body slouched to the ground.

She felt nothing. No remorse. No pleasure at seeing him dead. Nothing. She hurriedly wiped her gloves and the knife on his clothes and prepared herself to do it all over again. Claire ran down the hill, this time the knife tucked in the back of her trousers and her gloved hands in her pockets.

Don got out of the car. "Hey, where's Wayne?"

"He's admiring the view. Told me he'd take a walk while I give you your surprise. Do you want to join him or stay here with me?" She fluttered her eyelashes.

"Nope, it's too cold out there for me. It's nice and toasty in the car. My little man is ready for you." He glanced down at the bulge in his trousers.

"In the back then," she ordered, grinning broadly.

He grappled with the car door, his eagerness getting in the way of his brain functioning properly by the way he threw himself into the back seat.

"Get undressed, there's not much room in there to move otherwise."

He enthusiastically tore off his clothes. Claire smiled down at him. At least he had a trimmer figure than Wayne. Her mind raced. It was true, there wasn't much room in the back of the car. Doubts if she was doing the right thing swarmed her head.

"I'm ready," he said, playfully thrusting his hips in her direction, making his cock wave at her.

Claire battled the urge to vomit. Her mind on what she had to do, she slid into the car and grabbed his penis in her hand. Don immediately closed his eyes, anticipating what she was about to do next. He was wrong. She moaned and took the knife out; her aim was spot on. One swipe, and she was holding his member in her hand. His eyes flew open in horror.

"What the fuck?" he screamed.

She stabbed him in the stomach, slashing at his hands if they got in her way. "Call it revenge for all the times you've raped me and my sister. You disgust me. You're sick in the head. May you rot in Hell along with all the other depraved individuals down there. You've raped for the final time, scumbag. The world will be a better place without you in it."

"I...I...I'm sorry..." They were his final words as the light faded from his eyes and his head lolled to the side.

Her heart racing, she wiped the knife on his clothes piled up in the footwell and left the car. Claire took the weapon and the gloves back to her father's car and shoved them in the glove box. There were patches of blood on the base of her jumper. She slipped it off and hurled it in the boot of the car. Then she drove up the lane and found another pull-in. It took her six attempts to turn the car around. She should have dragged his body out of the car and up the track to avoid a stranger stumbling across it, but in truth, all she wanted to do was get back to see if Kathryn was okay. This had been the longest she'd left her alone with her father while he was awake. Her sister wasn't as strong as Claire; she was liable to come under attack if her father caught her sniffling or crying.

She arrived back at the cabin within five minutes. Her sister was standing on the front porch, tears in her eyes. She ran and hugged her. "Are you all right?"

"Yes. My God, what have you done?"

"What?" she asked, confused. She studied her sleeves and hands. There was nothing there.

"Your face. Is that blood?"

"Crap, help me to wipe it off, Kathryn. If father sees it, he'll kill me."

Together they cleaned her up just in time.

Her father stepped onto the porch moments later. "What's going on out here? Load the car up, and we'll set off."

"Yes, Father," Claire replied, grabbing her sister's hand and rushing through the door to the bedroom.

"Claire, what did you do?" Kathryn demanded in a hushed voice the second the door closed behind them.

"I punished them. They won't be raping any more women, I can assure you."

Her sister gasped and buried her head in her hands. "No, you didn't! That makes you as bad as them. I can't cope with this. When will it all end?"

"Soon. Please, don't judge me, Kathryn. I did it for you."

Her sister's hands dropped to reveal a startled expression. "Don't put this on me, Claire. You have money back at the house. All we had to do was collect that and escape. Why kill them?"

"There's not enough money to live on, not yet. I had to kill them. Please, don't hate me."

Kathryn stared at her. "I could never hate you. All you've tried to do in this world is protect me. I'll be forever in your debt for that, Claire."

Their father thumped on the door. "Come on. It's time to go. Get out here, you two."

Claire kissed her sister on the cheek. "Are you ready? Let's get this journey over and done with, then we can make more plans when we get home. I have a major one brewing."

"What about the two men? Where are their bodies?" Kathryn whispered.

"I didn't have time to do anything with them. They're down a lane. Hopefully, no one will find them for a while. We'd better get our skates on. Do you have everything?"

"I think so."

"What about the bathroom, anything left in there?"

"I checked earlier. Oh gosh, my mind is reeling. You'd better see for yourself."

She gripped Kathryn's shoulders firmly. "You have to act normally, love. Don't go freaking out on me, not now."

"Okay, I'll try. But those two men are dead."

"You need to get past it. Think of what we've had to contend with over the last couple of days, although I'd rather you didn't. It won't do you any good dwelling on things. We'll be free of this life soon, I promise you."

"I hope so. I love you so much, Claire. I'm not sure what I would have done if you'd left home years ago."

"Nonsense. You're my little sister. It's my duty to look after you. I'm just sorry we've had to suffer the way we have over the years."

Their father's voice thundered through the door. "My patience is wearing thin, and you know what happens when it does. Get a frigging move on. I want to get on the road."

"Come on. I know it's difficult, but try and put all this behind you during the journey." Claire was aware how much her sister tended to dwell on the terrible things that had blighted her life in the past, whereas she had the ability to shut the horrors out until nightfall descended and the nightmares began.

"I'll try."

They left the bedroom and were confronted by their angry father.

"Get in the car. You two are a bloody waste of space."

Except when we're shagging your friends! You'll get yours, old man, one day!

CHAPTER 11

LORNE TRAVELLED into work feeling utterly dejected. The previous couple of days had consisted of her and her team chasing their tails, not only around the office but through every computer system available to the police, and still they were left scratching their heads. Which was making Lorne doubt if they were pursuing the right angle to this case. Were they looking for a paedophile gang? All the signs were there. But they were sketchy. Nothing prominent sticking out as yet. There was still one man on the list, a Dave Dixon, who Lorne hadn't managed to track down to speak to yet, as he'd recently left the flat where he'd been living after his divorce had come through.

Katy was walking across the car park to the station's entrance when she arrived. Lorne tooted her horn, almost scaring the crap out of Katy who was intently studying her mobile phone.

"Bloody hell, Lorne. It's a bit early in the day to attempt to cause me a heart attack," Katy said sternly as she caught up with her.

"Oops, sorry. It brightened my dull day to see you nearly drop your phone. What's so interesting anyway?" She grabbed the iPhone out of Katy's hand and flicked through the messages. "Aww…AJ sending you little love poems? I wonder how long that will last. Mind you, he hasn't put a ring on your finger yet."

Katy glared and snatched the phone back. "He does not! If you must know, he sent me this." She angled the phone for Lorne to see. On the screen was a picture of her gorgeous daughter, Georgina, smiling whilst eating her breakfast.

"That's so sweet. Sorry for winding you up."

Katy had tears in her eyes. "I should be at home with her, watching these kinds of images in the flesh, not learning about them via a damn text message."

Lorne slung an arm around her shoulders and hugged her tight. "I appreciate how difficult this is and what lies ahead for you when I retire in a few days. I'm sorry for dropping you in it and making your life so damned miserable, love."

Katy turned and smiled at her. "You haven't. Please don't think I'm having a go at you because I'm not. I guess it's hard on all working mothers missing out on their children growing up. How did you cope, back in the day when Charlie was a toddler?"

They strode through the main door and up the stairs. "I just did. My problem, although I didn't see it as an issue at the time, was that I didn't have a maternal bone in my body. Therefore, I was super keen for Tom to do all the child-rearing. At times, over the years, I've regretted that decision so much. I have to give Tom the credit he deserves for the way Charlie has turned out. I know we had to go through a rough patch with her in her teens, but she pulled through that and came out the other side, with the intervention of the damned Unicorn, of course." She shuddered as the vile criminal's face entered her mind.

"Sorry, Lorne. I didn't mean to summon up the old memories for you. Are you okay?"

"I'm fine. Truth be told, I'm feeling a little down about the investigation anyway. It's been a trying couple of days. Can't say I slept very well last night either. Still, it's Friday, and we have a weekend ahead of us to look forward to."

"If things don't kick off. Aren't those men due back from their fishing trip today?"

"Yep, another reason why I couldn't sleep. I don't suppose they'll show up until late afternoon, though. That means we're in for a very long day, again."

"It will be, if you don't alter your attitude. It's a shame the police up north didn't put extra effort in to help us try and locate the men."

"It was an impossible task for them, given the amount of rental properties on the websites in that area. Anyway, if a job's worth doing, we tend to do it ourselves, don't we?"

"That's because we're the A-Team." Katy chuckled.

"For now. I hope I'm not leaving you in the lurch."

"You're not. No one deserves their retirement more than you do, Lorne. I'll survive; as a team, we'll survive. Don't be surprised if the phone in your office is red-hot to your home in Norfolk when you leave."

"I'll be upset if you don't ring me when you need some advice, love, although you're more than capable of running the team as well as I do. You've done it in the past."

"Yeah, and I seem to remember hating every damn minute of it. What the fuck am I doing?" She pulled her hair at the roots.

"Don't make me feel guiltier than I am already, please." Lorne laughed.

Once the morning rituals were out of the way, the rest of the day dragged past until Lorne received a disturbing call which came in at around three.

"DI Warner. How can I help?"

"This is DI Trent from the Cumbria Constabulary."

"Hello, DI Trent, what can I do for you? Oh, wait, don't say you've managed to locate the people we were enquiring about?"

"You could say that. A gentleman was walking his dog in a well-known hiking area, and he stumbled across a naked man. He'd been murdered."

"Shit! This man, did he have any ID on him or near him?"

"Yes, a Wayne Jethrum."

"Crap, yes, that's the man we were hoping to speak to regarding our ongoing investigation. Was he alone?"

"Funny you should ask that. The man who found him also stumbled across a car. We've since learnt that car is registered to a Don Barton."

"The other man we were interested in speaking to. Don't tell me he was found dead as well?"

"He was. Umm…minus his penis, although I'm guessing the stab wounds to his chest were the likely cause of death. Poor bugger, either way."

"Okay, well, the MO sounds similar to what we're dealing with in our investigation. I don't suppose this man saw another vehicle in the vicinity or any other walkers acting suspiciously, did he?"

"Nope, nothing. And we have no CCTV cameras around there. I've instructed my team to conduct house-to-house enquiries in the immediate area, and we've contacted the petrol station up the road to see if their CCTV has picked up the car. That'll take time to come through, sorry. Anything else you need from me?"

"No, nothing that I can think of at this stage. I'll let the families know. I take it that's why you're really ringing me?"

"Yes, it'll save me a trip down there. I prefer to stay away from the Big Smoke. I value my lungs too much."

Lorne sniggered. "It's not that bad. I'll visit the families right away. Thanks for the call."

"All in a day's work, Inspector. Can't say I'm that happy to have a couple of murders on our patch. I enjoy the quiet life in the country. This has put paid to that."

"Oh dear, we all have our crosses to bear." Lorne ended the call and took her notebook into the incident room where she relayed the information she'd been given to her team.

"Graham, it's a long shot, but can you try and track the other vehicle that we're interested in? See if you can pick it up on the ANPR cameras."

Katy cleared her throat. "Why? You think the Frost family is behind the murders?"

Lorne shrugged. "Your guess is as good as mine. You know how much I hate coincidences." Her arms flew out to the sides and dropped to slap against her thighs. "Crikey, we don't even know if they were heading in the same direction at the end of the day."

"Well, both cars were caught on the cameras heading up that way," Graham reminded them.

"Then we have to come to that conclusion, don't we? Katy, you and I have to go out and inform the families."

"How come we get to do all the crummy jobs?" Katy complained, slipping the jacket off the back of her chair and putting it on.

"Senior officers get all the perks, you should know that by now. I'll just get my jacket."

"Some perks are worth foregoing in my eyes."

Lorne smiled and shouted over her shoulder, "I hear ya, sister."

They decided to call at Wayne Jethrum's house first. Sandra opened the door and seemed surprised to see them again.

"Hello, Sandra. Would it be all right if we came in and spoke to you for a moment or two?"

"Of course. You're a little early. Wayne rang me just after breakfast this morning, told me they were going to take their time driving back. I suppose they'll be here around five or six. Who knows with those two?"

She led them into the lounge and gestured for them to take a seat.

Lorne perched on the edge of the sofa next to Katy and inhaled a large breath. "I'm sorry to have to tell you, Sandra, that we believe your husband has been murdered."

"What? What do you mean? He's on a fishing trip with Don, how could that be?"

"We've had a call from an officer with the Cumbria Constabulary to say that your husband and Don were both found murdered a few hours ago."

"No! I don't believe you. Let me ring him? This must be some kind of mistake."

Lorne left her seat and crossed the room. She sat on the arm of the chair Sandra was sitting in and rested an arm around her shoulders. "It's true. I'm sorry."

The devastated woman shook her head in disbelief. "But why? Who would want to kill him?"

"We've yet to find that out, Sandra. I'm not sure if you remember me telling you, when we visited a couple of days ago wanting to question Wayne, about an ongoing investigation?"

"Yes, you said two men had lost their lives. Oh, no, you're not telling me there's a connection, are you?"

"It would appear so, yes. Something to do with that list I mentioned we have in our possession. When I questioned your husband regarding the list over the phone, he told me it was to do with a bridge club. Obviously, after what has happened, we believe your husband probably lied to us. Any idea why he would do that?"

"No, not in the slightest. Murdered? Oh my. I can't believe it. Why Wayne? And Don for that matter? What were the names of these other men? Did you mention that last time? I can't remember." She placed a hand to her cheek which had drained of all colour. Shock was setting in.

"Denis Tallon and Larry Small. Did you know them?"

Sandra focussed on a patch of carpet in front of her. "No," she whispered.

"I'm so sorry to break such tragic news to you, Sandra. Is there someone we can call for you?"

"I think I need my sister here. It's just sinking in that I'll never see him again." Tears spilled down her cheeks. She wiped her nose on a tissue she'd plucked from a box sitting on the table beside her chair.

"Do you have your sister's number? Katy will give her a call for you."

Sandra grabbed her mobile, punched in a number and handed it to Katy who made the call in the hallway. Lorne tried to comfort Sandra, but the woman's sobs drowned out Lorne's words. Katy returned to the room and placed the mobile beside Sandra again.

"Your sister will be here within ten minutes."

"Thank you. Oh my God, how am I going to tell Wayne's parents?

They're both fragile and riddled with dementia. He was their only child."

"Maybe your sister can go with you. Perhaps the doctor in charge of their welfare will advise you not to tell them if they're that bad. I haven't had to deal with dementia in the past so I'm not really sure what to suggest for the best."

"I'll have a word with the doctor, that's a good idea."

They sat there in relative silence until the doorbell rang. Katy opened the door to let a chubby woman with blonde highlights running through her hair into the house. The sisters hugged each other tightly.

"Oh, Bridget, what am I going to do without him?"

"Hush now, love. We'll sort everything out, don't you fret. I'm so sorry this has happened, to you of all people. Poor Wayne." She turned to face Lorne. "Have you caught the person who is responsible for this yet?"

"No, not yet. Our colleagues up in Cumbria are dealing with the investigation at their end. We're dealing with a similar case here."

"Another murder?"

"Two. Two men who were acquainted with Wayne and his friend, Don, who also died today."

"Are we talking about a serial killer being on the loose?" Bridget asked, perplexed.

"Too early to say. Something isn't sitting right with us, though. Are you going to be all right, Sandra, now that your sister is here? Only we have to go and break the news to Don's wife now."

"I'll be fine. Will you pass on a message for me?"

"Of course, what's that?"

"Will you pass on that I'm thinking of her and if she wants to give me a call at any time, to feel free to do so?"

"I'll do that. Again, I'm sorry for your loss. I'll keep you up to date on how the investigation is going."

"Thank you."

Lorne and Katy left the house and drove to the next address. The atmosphere in the car was palpable, each of them wrapped up in their own thoughts.

"I'm not looking forward to telling Cathy Barton." Lorne parked up outside the bungalow they'd visited a few days before and they'd received a frosty reception. She could only imagine how the woman was going to react once she'd heard the news of her husband's death.

"No, neither am I. I hope she doesn't lash out. Before we go in, one thing is bugging me."

"What's that?"

"You spoke to Wayne the other day, and he was distracted whilst driving so was pretty abrupt with you, right?"

"Yep, that's true. What are you getting at?"

"Didn't the Cumbria police tell you they had traced Don's registration number when they found a car in the lane?"

"That's right. What's your point?"

"Would the two men have taken two cars? Logically, I don't think they would have. So why lie?"

"Hmm…I see what you're getting at now. Let's ask Mrs Barton if Wayne left his car here before they set off. I'm not sure what significance it will make to the case, but yes, if it turns out that Wayne was lying, we have to ask why."

They exited the car. Lorne felt a thousand butterflies—or were they the ugly moths she'd hated so much as a child?—take off in her stomach. "Are you ready for the onslaught?" she said out of the corner of her mouth.

"I'll get my cuffs ready, just in case she kicks off. Oh, the joys of being a London police off—"

The door was flung open, cutting Katy off mid-sentence.

"You! What do you pair want?" Cathy Barton slung at them with venom, closing the door a few inches.

"We're here on official business. May we come in, Mrs Barton?"

"No. Not without a warrant. Say what you have to say and get the hell off my property."

Lorne sighed and did just that. "It is with regret that I have to tell you that your husband was murdered this morning."

The woman tipped her head back and roared. "What a comedienne you are. I thought that the minute I laid eyes on you."

"It's true. Do you really want to continue this conversation outside on the doorstep or would you like us to come inside?"

Barton threw open the door. The handle bashed against the hall wall, knocking a coat off the rack behind the door. She marched ahead of Lorne and Katy and disappeared into the lounge, not uttering a word.

Lorne picked up the coat and threw it onto the rack and chased after her. Katy shut the front door behind her. They found Mrs Barton lighting up a cigarette, her hands shaking as she held the lighter.

"Just tell me where and get out of my house."

"Really? Is that how you want to play this, Mrs Barton?"

"I asked you a damn question. Either you answer it or I'll bloody report you to your superiors."

Lorne shrugged. "Up in Cumbria."

"Now get out."

"We're not going anywhere until we've asked a few questions. I'm getting the impression you're not totally surprised by your husband's demise. May I ask why?"

"No particular reason. You can go now."

"I have a few questions first, and then we'll leave."

"I ain't saying anything without a solicitor being present. I know how your lot like to bend the bloody truth when it suits you."

"We don't, but that's beside the point. Why all the aggression? Does it have something to do with the book we found at another victim's house?"

"What the sodding hell are you talking about, woman?"

"I think it does. Here's what I'm thinking: your husband, along with five other men found on a list, were part of a paedophile ring. My hunch is you found out about your husband's exploits and that's why you're not upset about his death. Good riddance to bad rubbish and all that. Am I right, Mrs Barton?"

The woman's mouth hung open for a little while until she took a long drag on her cigarette, then she flopped into the chair behind her.

"Smart arse. Yes, you're right. He confessed to me last week. Told me he'd been to the doctor's and was diagnosed with liver cancer. He wanted to go to Heaven with a clear conscience—they were his words, not mine. I beat him black and blue. I was sickened by what he told me. He said he regretted his actions and if he could take back what he'd done he would, in a heartbeat. I'm glad he's dead. Does that make me a bad person?"

"Not in my eyes. Did he tell you the ins and outs of what went on?"

"I put my hands over my ears when he started to tell me, I didn't want to know. It was as if he was treating it like a confessional in the bloody church. I couldn't give a toss. That's what this trip was all about, him getting out of my hair for a few days. I hate him. Can't stand the thought of him abusing children. I lived with that man for fifteen years and didn't know him at all. It sickens me that he slept with minors and then came home to share my bed." She gagged a little. "See, all I've wanted to do since he told me is bloody vomit. What is wrong with these frigging men? They're depraved; they have to be, don't they?"

Lorne and Katy sat in the two easy chairs available.

Although Lorne's suspicions about the men had been right, it was still a tough pill to swallow. "Can I ask why you didn't report your husband to the police, if, like you say, it upset you so much?"

"I've been toying with the idea. I was in a difficult situation with him being ill, surely you can understand that?" She puffed on her cigarette.

"Okay. Look, these past few days, do you think anything along the lines he told you about could have gone on up in Cumbria?"

Mrs Barton stared at Lorne. "Do you? Is that why someone killed him? Hang on a minute, he was with Wayne up there, wasn't he? Or was that a lie, too?"

"It is our understanding that the two men were together in Cumbria. Actually, they were both found murdered."

"Oh crap. Does his wife know?"

"Yes, we've just come from there. She asked me to pass on her condolences. She knows about the murders, but I didn't pick up that she knew about anything else. She was shocked that her husband had been killed, unlike you."

"Poor cow. Christ knows how she's going to frigging feel when it comes out in the press. It's going to, isn't it? These things always do."

"It's likely, yes. Did your husband take his car to Cumbria?" She knew the answer; she was testing the woman now.

"Yes, why?"

"Did Wayne take his car as well?"

"No, his car is sitting in our garage. I don't understand why you're asking that."

"Well, when I spoke to Wayne a few days ago, he was en route to Cumbria at the time, he specifically told me that he was driving."

"Maybe they took it in turns to drive."

"Maybe, not that it matters, it just seemed odd that he should lie. Perhaps you're right. We'll gloss over that for now. Going back to your husband's confession, did he tell you where these 'acts' took place?"

"He tried, but I told him I'd knife him if he said any more. I can't explain how much I hated him at that moment. When you think you know someone…when you've invested so much time into a relationship that proves to be worthless…" She held her head in her hands and shook it. "I don't think I'm ever going to get over this. I feel as abused as those kids. Is it so wrong to say that? Our whole marriage has been a sham. Look at me! Am I likely to find anyone else to care for me at my time of life…shit, would I even *want* someone after what that fucker did? Sorry, I've turned this into being about me. I didn't mean to do that."

Lorne smiled. "I completely understand where you're coming from. If it's any consolation, you still have this place. I take it he was insured?"

"Who the hell frigging knows. If I go digging through his paperwork—he took care of that side of things, you see—Jesus, what bloody horrors am I going to find?"

"Would you like us to go through the paperwork with you?"

"No. I'll hand it over to my solicitor. I suppose I should ask you what's happening about his murder, not that I really give a toss."

"It's still an ongoing investigation. We have another couple of names we have to make contact with on the list. Maybe they'll be able to hint at who they think the perpetrator is. Do you need us to call anyone to be with you?"

"No. I'm fine on my own. I'd rather not drag my family into this shit. I'm sorry for being so offhand with you, my head's been all over the place since I found out."

"No need to apologise. I will have to ask you to formally ID your husband when his body is transferred. It'll probably be a few days yet."

"God, do I have to? Can't you do it from a photo?"

"Maybe. I'll have a word with the pathologist. Perhaps she'll agree to do it from his medical or dental records if that will help."

"If you wouldn't mind. I'd like to wash my hands of him. His family can foot the expense of a burial; I'm not interested in the bastard any more."

"That's your prerogative. We'll get on then. Thanks for sharing the information with us. I realise how painful that was for you."

She walked with them to the front door. "What about the other bastard's car?"

"We'll get someone to collect it tomorrow, if that's okay?"

"Sure."

They left the house and returned to the car.

Katy leaned back against the headrest. "Wow, that was quite a switch in character if ever I saw one."

"Yep. One thing is puzzling me: why she was so offensive last time towards us and yet this time…"

"Yeah, I thought the same. Maybe she's had time to reconsider her actions."

"Or the relief of being told he'd been murdered helped to make up her mind."

"Possibly. Either way, she's well rid of him by the sounds of it."

"I agree. Let's see if the Frosts are back now."

Lorne had just started the engine when her mobile rang. "DI Lorne Warner. How can I help?"

"Hello, dear. This is Gladys Lewis speaking, the Frosts' neighbour. You asked me to ring you when they returned, do you remember?"

"I do indeed, Mrs Lewis. I take it they're back now?"

"They are, dear. Just thought I'd give you a little tinkle to let you know."

"That's very kind. We're on our way now. Thank you for the call."

"You're most welcome. Goodbye, dear."

"Goodbye, Mrs. Lewis." Lorne pressed the End Call button and smiled at Katy. "Fortune always favours the brave, or something like that."

They both laughed, relieving the tension a little.

ARRIVING at the terraced house belonging to the Frosts, Lorne spotted the back of a female entering the front door of the property.

"She must be still unloading the car. Mrs Lewis was really quick to ring us."

"Looks that way. Do you want to sit here for a second longer?"

"Nope. Let's get this over with."

They made their way up the cracked path in the dingy, overgrown front garden, and Lorne used the cuff of her jacket to ring the bell for the second time that week. The young woman whom they'd seen entering the house opened the door. Lorne met her gaze. She appeared startled.

Lorne smiled warmly. "Miss Frost, we're DI Warner and DS Foster from the Met Police. May we come in and speak to your father?"

The woman nodded and stood behind the door, allowing them access to the hallway. The inside of the house was as shoddy as the outside. Drab wallpaper peeling at the edges lined the walls in the hallway. The young woman, still without saying a word, led them into the lounge. Sitting in a worn easy chair was a man in his late fifties to early sixties, reading a newspaper. He glanced up and jumped to his feet when he saw them enter the room. He glared at the female, as if to question why she had let them in. Lorne watched the exchange with interest as another female, this one younger, joined them.

"Who are you?" Mr Frost demanded.

Lorne held up her warrant card. He peered over the top of his glasses to read it. "DI Lorne Warner. We'd like to ask you a few questions if you don't mind, Mr Frost. Take a seat. Girls, would you take a seat also, please?"

Mr Frost shuffled back to his chair, and his daughters sat on the sofa on the other side of the room, their thighs and arms touching.

"What's this intrusion about?" he asked.

"Maybe you can start by telling us where you've been the last few days, Mr Frost."

"Up to the Lakes. Why?" His brow wrinkled when he replied.

"Just the three of you?"

"Yes, a family break. I'm sorry, what does this have to do with you?"

"Did anyone go with you?"

"Just the three of us—well, a couple of friends stayed in a separate cabin, and we met up with each other a few times to share the odd meal and a drink. You know how it is when you're on holiday."

"Did you have a good time?" Lorne directed her question at the two daughters.

"Yes, thank you. It was a nice rest," the girl who'd let them in replied.

"Good. What about you?" Lorne asked the other girl.

Her gaze drifted over to her father.

He gestured with his hand for her to hurry up.

"Yes, it was a beautiful area."

"These friends you mentioned, could you tell me their names, sir?"

"I don't understand. Why should I? Have we broken a law or something?"

"Not as far as I know. Their names, Mr Frost?"

"Wayne and Don, can't remember their surnames."

"Girls, do you know their full names?" Again, Lorne watched the interaction between the father and his daughters, and something didn't sit right with her.

"No. Sorry, we don't," the older one said after they'd briefly conferred.

"Ah, I see. Good friends, but you don't remember their names."

"Meaning what?" Frost snapped.

"Nothing, just stating facts, sir. Perhaps you can tell me how long you've known these men, or would your bad memory have a problem with that?"

"What are you getting at? Of course I remember. Over twenty years."

"I see. Did you set off together this morning, or did Wayne and Don leave their cabin after you?"

"Actually, they left before. What's this all about? Why are you asking about my mates?"

"And they seemed okay when they left?"

"Yes. Looking forward to going home to see their wives."

"I see. Both of them?"

"Yes," Frost said, his irritation growing.

"Only we heard some disturbing news from one of the wives this afternoon."

"About what?"

"Something we need to investigate further before we're willing to share it publicly. So, Wayne and Don set off before you this morning. Did you catch up with them on the road at a service station or something?"

"No. What kind of question is that? Is it likely, given they set off a good half an hour before us?"

"Ah, that makes sense."

"Look, are you going to be long? We've had a heck of a trip, and the girls are keen to get on with dinner."

"Sorry, not long now. I wanted to know something specific before we leave. Do you know a Denis Tallon and a Larry Small?"

"Yes, as it happens, they're good buddies of mine. Why?"

"We're conducting an investigation into their murders."

Frost flung his newspaper off the side of his chair and got to his feet. "What? Both of them? That's incredible. How?"

"We're not prepared to go into detail just now. As a close friend of theirs, we wondered if you knew of anyone who might have had a grudge against these two men."

"No. Not at all. They were decent chaps. The girls will tell you, won't you, girls?"

The girls glanced at each other briefly and then back at Lorne.

"Yes, both nice," the older one confirmed, a little grudgingly to Lorne's ear.

"The truth is, we're looking for a possible motive for the murders. Do you have an idea why someone would want both those men dead, Mr Frost?"

"What am I, the bloody Oracle? I haven't got a damn clue."

"Okay, we'll leave it there then. Here's my card if ever you need to talk to me about anything that's troubling you, or if you can think of a reason why someone would want to kill your friends, all four of them. Ring me day or night, I'm always available." She watched his eyes narrow when she mentioned the four friends' deaths but decided to leave it there, for now. Lorne handed all three of them a card and smiled at Katy. "We have work to do, partner, back at the station. Let's leave these nice people to get settled after their arduous trip."

Katy nodded and walked into the hallway.

"It was nice meeting you all. Sorry it was under difficult circumstances." Lorne followed Katy out of the room then the front door.

They left the garden, and before Lorne could get in the car, Mr Frost erupted inside the house.

"Whoa! Are you just going to walk away and let him get away with that, Lorne?" Katy demanded, staring back at the house.

"We have no reason to interfere, Katy. Get in the car. We need to get back to base and do some digging."

Katy had a disappointed expression on her face when she turned to look at her. "You're the boss."

"For now," Lorne replied and slid behind the steering wheel.

CHAPTER 12

As soon as the policewomen left the house, Claire was set upon by her father, his stride full of menacing intent as he stormed across the floor towards her and her sister. Kathryn was trembling so hard beside her that her teeth chattered.

"You," her father bellowed. "I know you did this somehow."

"I didn't, Father, you never let us out of the house. How could either of us do it?"

"I don't know, but I know you're behind their deaths. All of them. How could you?"

She shook her head, avoiding eye contact with him, which was difficult when his face was only a few inches from her own. She swallowed down the acid taste filling her mouth and squeezed Kathryn's hand tightly.

Her father tore away from them and paced the living room carpet, running a hand through his hair and simultaneously growling, his anger clearly mounting.

"I'll make us a cup of coffee, you've had a shock," Claire said, her voice hushed so as not to anger him even more.

Her father lashed out, yelling profanities at the pair of them. His fist connected with Claire's jaw. The blow was so violent that her head smacked into her sister's.

Her father smiled, pleased with his actions. "Two birds with one stone." He sniggered and fell into his chair. "Fetch me a glass and the bottle of whisky. I want to raise a toast to my dearly departed friends."

Claire placed a hand to her jaw, wiggled it from side to side to ensure nothing was broken and ran into the kitchen. She didn't want to be too long for Kathryn's sake. She collected a glass and the alcohol her father had requested and dashed back to the lounge.

Her father snatched the items from her hand. "Now, what's for dinner? I'm starving."

"I thought I'd make cottage pie, if that's all right, Father?" Claire mumbled.

"Whatever. Get it done and be quick about it. This will suffice for now."

"Kathryn, can you help me prepare the vegetables?"

Her sister shot out of her chair, eager to join her.

When they were both safely tucked away in the kitchen, Kathryn crumpled into a chair and placed her head on her arm on the table.

Claire ran a soothing hand over her head. "We can do this. Ignore him. I know how difficult that is at times. I have your back."

Kathryn glanced up at her. "We need to get out of here, Claire. Those policewomen will be back. I'm sure they know."

"They won't. You're reading things into it, love."

Kathryn's head swished from side to side. "I don't think so. The main one, she had a glint in her eye. I think she's more intelligent than she looked."

"I think you're wrong. They barely asked any questions. If they'd suspected anything, they would have insisted on us joining them at the station to be interviewed. Enough of this. We need to get on with dinner before he starts on the warpath. Are you all right?"

"No. I'm a quivering wreck. I can't cope with this situation any longer. We need to get away, Claire, soon."

Claire tapped her temple. "I have it all sussed out. I need to get my timings right, love. Bear with me a little while longer."

"I fear we're running out of time. Those coppers will be back soon, mark my words on that one."

"We'll see. Now, what do you fancy, cauliflower and peas or carrots and peas?"

"I don't give a shit. I doubt he's going to allow us to eat anything anyway, not now we're back here. It was different while we were away, in front of those men. He let us eat normally to make him look good. That man commented on how thin we both were. I told him our metabolism was messed up and that we ate a lot and never gained weight."

Claire touched her sister's face. "See, good girl, we have to keep up the pretence. People wouldn't believe what we've had to contend with over the years."

Between them, they organised the dinner. Claire fried off the minced meat with the onion, thickened the gravy and covered it with mashed potato. After placing the casserole dish in the oven, she eased open the door to the lounge to see what her father was up to. He was asleep in the chair. An overwhelming sense of relief washed over her. They could relax for the next half an hour or so. In that time, a plan formulated. They would eat dinner early and then allow their father to hit the bottle again after the meal while they cleaned up the kitchen and then went to their room for the evening.

Once her father was asleep, replete from his meal, and they were back in the bedroom, then she would put the finishing touches to her plan. First, she needed to sneak into the lounge to get her father's address book out of the cupboard behind him. That was going to be tricky. If he caught her, he'd crucify her.

"I won't be a second. Keep an eye on dinner for me." She tiptoed into the lounge and slunk past her father, pausing in case he sensed her brush past him. When he didn't wake, she opened the door to the old pine cupboard, fearful that the catch would give her away. It didn't. She extracted her father's phone book and closed the door again, then she retraced her steps to the kitchen, taking the phone with her.

Kathryn frowned when Claire squeezed past her and went out into the garden. She rang a number and waited for the call to be answered. "Hello there, is it possible to speak to Mr Dixon, please?"

"Just a moment, I'll see if he's available. What's the name please?"

"Claire Frost, he's an old family friend." She almost choked on the word *friend*.

"Hold the line."

Claire marched down the path a little way and turned back quickly, remembering the phone's range.

"Putting you through now, Miss Frost," the female said, coming back on the line.

"Thank you."

"Claire, is that you?"

"Yes, Mr Dixon. I need to see you on an urgent matter."

"What's wrong?"

"Can you see me today, after work?"

"Of course. I can hang around here until six. Drop by the bank. Is your father okay?"

"Not really, that's why I need to see you. For advice really, financial advice."

"Oh, I see. Of course. I'll see you later."

"I appreciate it. Bye for now." Claire ended the call and let out a relieved breath. She checked the time on the kitchen clock as she entered the back door. It was cutting it a bit fine. She had an hour to complete the meal, serve and eat it, and pray her father fell asleep in the chair again, enabling her to slip out and be at the bank for six. *Shit! What was I thinking? I'll never make it.* She had to.

She relayed the information to Kathryn at the same time she took the casserole dish from the oven and placed it in the microwave to hurry the cooking along, then she returned to the stove and upped the flames under the gas to cook the vegetables quicker.

"Get the cutlery ready, Kathryn. We need to get things organised, and I need to get father fed and asleep again by five forty-five at the latest."

"There's no way that's going to happen."

Claire came up with another idea. She went to the kitchen drawer and found a few sleeping tablets her father had been prescribed months ago. She crushed three of them up with a rolling pin, ready to add to his meal once it was dished up.

Ten minutes later, her father was sitting in his chair eating his enormous meal, laced with the pills, and Kathryn and Claire were sitting at the kitchen table sharing out the scraps her father had kindly left them.

The girls cleared up the kitchen. Claire collected her father's plate and poured him another glass of whisky.

"Are you trying to get me drunk?" her father barked at her.

"No, Father. It's been a long day travelling. Just trying to help you unwind a little. Kathryn and I will clear up the kitchen and go to our rooms. Goodnight."

He mumbled a 'night' and took a large swig from his glass. Claire went back into the kitchen, her gaze darting up at the clock, her heart racing at what was to come—if she could get out of the house in time.

She left it another five minutes and then poked her head around the door. Her father's chin was resting on his chest, his glass tilting in his hand, spilling the amber liquid. She closed the door and thumped the air. "Thank God, he's asleep. I need to get a move on."

"Are you going dressed like that?" Kathryn pointed at the jeans and T-shirt Claire had been dressed in all day.

"Shit. I'll fling a dress on, look the part. Two minutes." She flew upstairs, being careful not to step on a squeaky stair on her way up and when she came back down again.

Kathryn smiled. "You're so pretty when you wear a dress."

Claire hugged her sister and kissed her cheek. "Go to the bedroom, in case he wakes up. I told him we were going to our room after dinner. He'll think we're asleep. I won't be long."

"Good luck. I love you, Claire."

"I know you do, sweetie. I'll nip out the back door. Will you leave it open for me?"

"Of course I will. Stay safe. Don't put yourself in any danger. If the situation doesn't feel right, you'll get out of there, promise me?"

"I will. Don't worry about me."

Claire left the back door and sprinted up the alley beside the house. The bank was a five-minute walk away. The more she rushed, the more she wobbled on her three-inch heels. She wasn't used to wearing them. Stuck to jeans and trainers mostly, less chance of being groped by her father. Her bag chafed her thigh as she moved.

Peering through the window of the bank, she spotted Dave Dixon at the end of the corridor behind the counter. She tapped on the window to draw his attention. He waved, dipped into an office and came back into the hallway with a bunch of keys in his hand. Unlocking the door, he welcomed her.

"Hello, stranger. My, don't you look pretty. It's been a while since I've had the pleasure of your delightful company. I was thrilled to receive your call."

She pasted a smile in place and gushed, "You're my last resort, Mr Dixon. Dad is at his wit's end with money problems. I'll do anything I can to get him out of a fix. Can you help?"

"Of course. Come through to my office." He slung an arm around her bare, slender shoulders, and they walked up the corridor to his office, side by side.

Once inside, he took her in his arms and kissed her. A wet, eager kiss that turned her stomach. She pulled away from him, still clutching her handbag, ready to dip inside it when the time came.

"I'm sorry. Business first and pleasure after."

He stepped back and perched his backside on the desk, holding out a hand for her to take. She slipped her hand into his, and he pulled her closer, settling her between his thighs.

"What do you need?"

"Father needs a new car. Around twenty grand?"

"Whoa! I can't sanction an amount like that. Your father will have to make an appointment with our loan advisor. We need to do this above board, Claire. Otherwise, I risk getting the sack."

She smiled and opened her bag. Drawing out a knife with a ten-inch blade, she placed it to his throat. "No chance of you reconsidering that, Dave?"

His Adam's apple bobbed up and down. "Wait just a damn minute. You can't do this, Claire."

She glared at him. "Can't I? Who says? After the despicable things you've made me do over the years, I think I'm entitled to a little extra money. Open the safe."

His arm came up, tried to grab hers. But she swiftly cottoned on to what his intentions were.

"Don't even try it." The knife nicked his throat.

"Ouch. That hurt."

"I warned you. Don't mess with me. Where's the safe?"

"It's on a timer at this time of night, extra security to prevent things like this from happening."

"Don't give me that bullshit. Open it, now!"

He shrugged. "Don't say I didn't warn you. You'll need to give me room to move. The safe is next door."

"No funny business. I've already killed four men this week."

He pushed off the desk and froze. "What? Why?"

"Never you mind why. Just do as instructed, and you won't get hurt."

He gulped and walked out of the room with her less than a foot behind him. He bent down on one knee and opened the safe. Immediately, an alarm sounded.

"Shut it off. Do it, or I'll kill you."

"I warned you, I can't shut it off."

"Put the money in a bag, quickly."

Dixon picked up a canvas bag lying on the floor beside the safe and placed a few piles of cash into it.

"All of it," she ordered, her pulse racing and her head pounding against the noise. She was aware of the urgency to get out of there. The police would be there soon.

He inserted the final bundle of notes in the bag and stood.

She snatched the bag from his hand and plunged the knife into his stomach over and over again. "That's for all the times you poked me with your dick, you evil bastard. May the Devil make your afterlife hell when you get there."

He fell to the floor, blood seeping out of the side of his mouth. One question on his lips, "Why?"

She shook her head. There was no point going over it all with him now. Some men didn't know right from wrong in this world. She ran to the front door, grateful to find the keys still in the lock. The coast was clear by the look of things. She ran from the building and up a nearby alley, thankful that no one saw her emerge from the building.

A man was in the alley, walking towards her. She dipped her head, pretending to be looking for something in her bag, her hand on the knife in case he stopped her. He didn't. She ran all the way home. Not caring what she was doing any more, now that she had more cash than she and Kathryn would ever need, she slipped into the lounge and raised the knife. Her father must have sensed her near him. His eyes flew open.

"What the…?"

He didn't get the chance to say anything else. The knife jabbed him in the heart, not once but a thousand times—at least that was what it felt like to Claire. She tore off her shoes and bolted up the stairs.

"Kathryn. Get packed. We're leaving."

"You got the money? How?"

"It doesn't matter. Move it, we don't have much time."

"Why? Oh shit! Did you kill him?"

"He deserved it, love. They all did." She ripped off her dress, took out the only other pair of jeans she possessed, stepped into them then filled the holdall her sister had unpacked in her absence with all her worldly goods. There wasn't much to pack. Then she helped Kathryn do the same, eager to get away from the house.

Kathryn was crying as she filled the bag, snot mixing with her tears. "I want to go, but I don't want to leave him. He needs us, Claire. He's always needed us."

Claire pointed to the bruise coming out on her chin. "He needs us as a punchbag and to cook and clean for him, not forgetting to be his prostitutes. Wake up, Kathryn. We'll be better off without him. We have to go, now."

"But I haven't finished," Kathryn sniffled.

"I need to get the other money out of the loft." Claire went in search of the chair in her father's bedroom, the smell of his disgusting BO attacking her nostrils when she entered the room. They'd both be better off without him. The chair bashed against her leg on the journey back into the hallway. She placed it beneath the hatch and stood on it. The door swung open. She reached in and grabbed the bag she'd stashed there a few days before.

Kathryn joined her on the landing. "I'm ready."

"Good. Let's go. I have the other money downstairs. We'll go out the back way."

Kathryn's eyes filled with tears. "I want to see him one final time."

"No. I can't let you. It's better if we leave now, love."

Kathryn barged past her into the lounge and let out a scream that sent a shudder shooting down Claire's spine. "Why? What did you do, Claire?"

"What I had to do to get us away from him. We need to go." Claire dragged her sister by the arm.

Kathryn dug her heels in.

"Fine, stay here, if that's what you want. I'll go by myself."

"No. I'll come. Don't leave me," her sister pleaded, apparently having a sudden change of heart.

CHAPTER 13

IT HAD BEEN all systems go for Lorne and Katy since they returned to the station. Lorne had prioritised a warrant for the Frosts' address. Something didn't sit right with her there. She was eager to take a proper look around their house to find more evidence. As it stood, having the notebook with the list of names, and Isaac Frost being on that list with all the other people mentioned now lying on slabs in the mortuary, it was imperative for Lorne to find out more. Was Isaac behind the murders? Or someone else in the Frost household perhaps?

The team had looked into the family's background, but nothing had shown up so far. Lorne had an inkling the two daughters were hiding something. Either they were used in the paedophile gang's activities or they knew who had killed the men. She wasn't sure which way to turn on that score yet.

Time was getting on. Lorne felt weary now. She had a feeling the warrant wouldn't come through until possibly Monday. She'd already rung Tony, warning him it would be likely she'd have to put in several hours of overtime over the weekend.

"Okay, team. I think we've done well today. Why don't we call it a day?"

The team agreed and switched off their computers.

"Are you working tomorrow?" Katy asked on their way out of the incident room, turning off the lights.

"Yep, I'll come in for a few hours. No point all of us giving up our weekend."

"A trooper until the end, eh, Lorne?"

"I think I'll have 'she gave it her all' written on my gravestone."

Katy laughed.

Lorne's attention was drawn ahead of them as they descended the stairs. There was a lot of activity going on around the reception area.

"Everything all right, Mick?" she asked the desk sergeant.

"Just organising my lads, ma'am. Are you off for the day?"

Something in the way he'd asked set her pulse racing. "I was. What's up?"

"Don't get involved, Lorne, we've done our bit for the day," Katy interrupted.

"Ignore her. Go on, Mick."

"We've got a reported murder at a bank, ma'am. My lads are down there now. SOCO are on their way."

"A bank robbery?"

"Appears to be," Mick replied anxiously.

"Okay, I'm intrigued enough to go over there and find out for myself. Which bank?"

"Barclays. Here's the address."

Lorne smiled. "You knew I wouldn't be able to resist, didn't you?"

Mick grinned at her. "I was hoping."

Lorne turned to Katy. "You go home to AJ if you want, I'll be fine."

"Are you sure? No, don't answer that, I know how disappointed you'll be in me if I don't tag along. So, guess what?"

They rushed out to the car and used the siren to guide them through the rush hour traffic, some parts of which were at a standstill.

Four police cars, an ambulance and the SOCO van were already at the scene when they arrived. Patti was at the van, stepping into her protective clothing.

"Hi. Have you been in there?" Lorne asked, ripping the plastic bag off a coverall and slipping it on.

Katy did the same.

"I wasn't expecting you. Yep, it's not pretty."

Fully protected from head to foot, the three of them entered the bank together. There was a young man in jeans and a T-shirt looking shell-shocked just inside the front door. He was in the process of giving a statement to a uniformed officer who was on the ball, Lorne was pleased to see.

"He's the assistant manager. Finished work about half an hour ago and came back when the alarm company informed him the alarm was going off. They couldn't reach the manager because he was here, so the young'un was the next on the list," Patti told them.

They followed Patti into an office where the manager was lying on the floor, his white shirt stained with his blood.

"Watch the vomit," Patti pointed out unnecessarily. "The assistant obviously doesn't have the stomach for murder."

"Who does?" Lorne replied.

Patti rolled her eyes. "True. Okay, as you can see, the safe is open. There's no money left inside."

"Have you spoken to the assistant at all?" Lorne asked.

"Not really. He couldn't tell me any more than that his boss was working late, finishing up some important paperwork that head office required urgently."

"How did the killer get in? Is there a back door?"

"My guess is that either the person made an appointment to worm their way in or he possibly let them in for some reason. Maybe the cameras will give us the answer."

Lorne nodded. "I'm going to have a word with the assistant. Be right back."

She and Katy returned to the front door. "Hello, Mr...?"

"It's Will Patching."

"Thank you. I'm DI Lorne Warner, and this is my partner, DS Katy Foster. Sorry to meet under such upsetting circumstances, and forgive me for getting straight to the point, but it's imperative we try and stop the perpetrator ASAP. The cameras, are they working?"

His eyes widened. "God, I should have thought of that. Yes, they should be, unless someone switched them off. Want me to check?"

"If you would. We'll come with you."

Will tore up the hallway and into the room opposite to where his boss's life had ended. He fiddled with the equipment and reversed the CD that had been recording.

Lorne gasped when she saw the figure of a woman speaking to the bank manager in the reception area. "Oh crap," she whispered when the angle changed and the camera zoomed in on the woman's face.

"Oh crap indeed," Katy said, clearly equally numb by what she was witnessing.

"Can you fast-forward the disc?" Lorne asked the assistant.

After viewing the next five minutes on the screen, Lorne had seen enough. "Come on, Katy, we need to go."

"Wait. Do you know this person?" Will asked.

"Yes. Thanks for your help. We'll be in touch soon."

She and Katy raced out to the car, and Lorne spotted another man speaking with a uniformed officer.

"Just a tick." Lorne reached the man and the officer within seconds. "Did you see something, sir?" she asked the man, flashing her ID.

"Not really. I was telling the officer here that I passed a young woman in the alley there. She was carrying a canvas bag."

"Which way was she heading?"

"Away from the bank."

"Thank you. Get the man's statement down, we'll chase it up soon," she instructed the officer.

They returned to the car and Katy drove to the Frosts' address. En route, Lorne rang the station and requested backup to meet them at the house. Another patrol car arrived the same time they did.

"We need to be careful, lads. The occupants could be armed and dangerous," Lorne warned.

"Want to wait for an Armed Response Team?" Katy suggested.

"That could take hours. We're all wearing stab vests, let's take a punt."

Katy yanked on Lorne's arm and pointed to the neighbour hanging over the hedge between the two houses.

Lorne approached the woman, keeping an eye on the Frosts' house at the same time. "Hello, Mrs Lewis. Can we help?"

"Hello again. When you left earlier there was an almighty ruckus inside, lots of shouting. Thought I heard a few yelps from the girls as if he'd struck them."

"Okay. Have you seen anyone leave the house since?"

"Yes, the two girls. I reckon they've had enough of their old man and left him."

"What makes you think that?"

"They took the car—not before they loaded it up with a few bags, though. Why would they do that when they've only just got back off holiday?"

"Why indeed. Thanks for your help. Please, go back inside. Things might get a little hairy around here in a moment."

"Oh dear. Thanks for the warning." The old lady scampered inside her house and slammed the front door shut behind her.

Katy nudged her arm. "What are you thinking?"

"That we need to get in there, warrant or no warrant."

Two uniformed officers were lingering close by.

"Break the door down."

The larger of the two men shoulder-charged the door, and it gave way on the first attempt.

Lorne followed the officers into the lounge and immediately urged them back outside. "Cordon it off as a murder scene."

"Shit," Katy said. "What about the girls?"

Lorne was already on the phone to the station. "Mick, get me a location on a vehicle as soon as you can."

"Reg number, ma'am?"

"I don't know, you'll have to look it up. The car will be registered to an Isaac Frost of five Goodall Road. Be quick, man."

"On it now, ma'am. Want me to call you back when I have the

info?"

"Do that." Lorne hung up and raked a hand through her hair. "Damn, I had a feeling I should have trusted my gut."

"What? You thought the girls were the killers?"

"No, not that as such, but something wasn't sitting right with me. Bugger." Her phone rang.

"Ma'am, we've got a location on the vehicle. It's fifteen miles from where you are now. Want me to get a patrol car to pull it over?"

"Not yet, give me the location. I'll shoot over there. Tell your lot to keep the car under observation for now. Give them my phone number and tell them to keep in touch."

"Will do, ma'am. Good luck."

She ended the call, bolted back to the car with Katy and set off. "Shit, my stomach hurts."

"Have you got any painkillers in your bag?"

Lorne searched her bag with her fingers crossed. "Phew, yes. Can I have a swig of your water?"

"Go for it. I hope it doesn't taste tainted, it's a few days old."

Lorne grabbed the bottle from the centre console, popped the pill and washed it down with the water. She shuddered as the pill eased down her throat.

Katy again used the siren, and within a few minutes they received a call from the car tailing the Frosts.

"Yes, where are you?"

"Coming up to the junction for the M1, ma'am. Want us to intervene before they join it?"

"You're going to have to. We're five minutes away."

"Roger that, ma'am."

Lorne ended the call and rested her head back against the seat. "Shit, I really am getting too old for this malarkey."

"No, you're not. Once the pain subsides, you'll be raring to go again." Katy swerved around a car dawdling on the open road ahead of them. "Bloody Sunday drivers. Wrong day of the week, love," she shouted, looking at the car in her mirror.

"Get us there in one piece, but put your foot down," Lorne ordered, the pain subsiding in her tummy. Her phone rang again.

"Ma'am, it's PC Jobbs. We've used a stinger and stopped the car. Two women are inside the vehicle."

"Okay, we're here now. We'll take over."

Katy yanked on the handbrake, and they leapt out of the car to join the uniformed officers trying to persuade the girls to leave the vehicle.

Lorne's gaze fixed on Claire's.

She finally opened the window to speak with her. "You, you have to help us."

"Why, what have you done, Claire?"

"We want to leave. These officers won't allow us to do that."

"Why do you want to leave?"

"Kathryn and I are going to start a new life."

"A new life, now that your father is dead?"

"You know?"

Lorne nodded. "All the names on that list are now dead, aren't they, Claire, and you did it, am I right?"

Claire bowed her head in shame. "They deserved it."

"Why? What did they do to you?"

Claire shook her head slowly. "I can't say it. I live with the nightmares every day. I had to prevent myself from going insane. Kathryn had nothing to do with the murders. I used to sneak out when father was asleep. Please, you don't know what we've had to contend with over the years at the hands of these men."

"You have my word that we'll try and get a deal for you, Claire. You were in an intolerable situation, one that most people wouldn't have survived."

Tears puddled onto her cheek. "Our mother left us with him, and he…he pimped us out. Starved us most of the time. I had to protect us. Kathryn needed protecting, and I was only too happy to take on that responsibility when I was younger."

"I admire you for sticking up for your sister; however, you still killed the abusers, Claire. That will carry consequences. Get out of the car, please."

Claire glanced at her sister. Kathryn nodded and began sobbing. Claire opened the door and stepped out. One of the officers rushed to put the cuffs on her.

"Hey, take it easy, she's suffered enough." Lorne smiled at Claire, an understanding of what it was like to be raped swimming through her.

Claire travelled with the uniformed officers while Kathryn rode back to the station with Katy and Lorne. The car was silent except for the sound of Kathryn crying in the back. Lorne swallowed down the knot of emotion tearing at her throat.

She meant what she'd said. She would do anything in her power to ensure the girls got a lesser sentence—if Kathryn was charged, that was debatable given the evidence against her.

EPILOGUE

THE INTERVIEWS with Claire and her sister proved to be both revealing and heartbreaking at the same time. Lorne spent most of the time emotionally wrought and on the verge of tears. It was evident that not only Claire's spirit had been broken by these despicable men, but her whole life had been destroyed beyond recognition.

As for her sister, Kathryn, it would appear that Claire had sacrificed so much more in order to protect her. Lorne figured that had the men only abused Claire from a young age, she could have lived with that and not have been tempted to set out on a trail of revenge. Claire revealed how devastated she'd felt the first time her sister had been raped. She'd almost slit her own wrists with her father's razor blade but didn't have the courage to leave her sister, knowing what the bastards would do to Kathryn if she wasn't around to fend them off.

To Lorne, there were two types of serial killer in operation in this world: the predatory serial killers and those who became serial killers out of necessity. The only way they could save their own lives was to rob the people, who had either raped or abused them over the years, of their own. Which left Lorne wondering how many more Claires there were in this world who had been driven to such lengths to free themselves.

Lorne's heart went out to the girls as she and Katy watched them being loaded up in the van and heading off to the remand centre. What a contrast this had been to the previous case where the perpetrator had knifed her, putting her in hospital. Claire and her sister seemed decent enough people who'd been driven to kill by the circumstances inflicted upon them by their own wicked father. She would do everything in her power to get that message across to the Crown Prosecution Service, if it was the last thing she ever did as a serving police officer in the Met.

The team's celebrations at the pub that night had been somewhat subdued, everyone realising what tragic conditions the girls must have lived in all their lives.

Even Sean Roberts was quiet at the pub that night.

Lorne leaned over and whispered in his ear, "Are you okay?"

He turned and smiled at her. "I suppose so. More upset about saying goodbye to you if you must know."

"I'll still be on the end of the phone, Sean. It's time I moved on. Solving this case has taught me that."

"We'll miss you. I know you've resigned in the past and come back. Retirement is different, though. There's no going back this time, Lorne. I just want to emphasise that point to you."

She smiled. "I appreciate your concern. There's no need for you to worry. Tony and I are definitely doing the right thing going to Norfolk."

He raised a glass and shouted, "To Lorne Simpkins/Warner, one of the best coppers the Met has ever had the fortune of having."

She blushed as the whole team stood and raised their glasses amidst, "To the guvnor, to the boss," from all the team except Katy.

She was staring at Lorne with tears welling up. "To my dearest friend and colleague, you'll be sorely missed."

Those words set them both off.

Lorne hugged Katy hard. "You'll go on to fill my shoes, love. I have no doubt about that."

Half an hour later, and Lorne said her farewells to her team. She left the group, throwing over her shoulder, "Don't forget the barbecue on Sunday, folks. I'm looking forward to meeting all your families."

Sean's head dropped, and Lorne groaned, realising she hadn't invited him because of the debacle with the retirement form.

"You know the address, Sean. Two o'clock at our gaff."

His gaze met hers. He beamed and raised his glass. "I'll be there."

On the drive home, Lorne struggled to hold back the tears. When she walked through the back door of the house, Tony rushed across the room and hugged her.

"My God, are you all right? Is it your stomach?"

"No. I'm fine. Me being foolish, that's all."

"Ah, I get it. Your final farewell drink with the team."

"Yep, one never to be repeated," she replied sullenly.

"You'll see them all in a few days. Let's make this barbecue one they'll never forget. The forecast is good, and I began buying the food today, trying to get ahead."

"You're amazing. Thank you, love."

They shared the longest of kisses.

It was chaotic on Sunday morning. Charlie and Brandon arrived around ten to lend them a hand with setting up the barbecue and all the tables outside in the paddock. Tony was right, the sun was ensuring that the day was a glorious one from the outset.

Everything was in place for when the guests started turning up at five minutes to two. Katy, AJ and Georgina were the first to arrive.

Lorne found it an emotional day but also one filled with love and happiness.

Somewhere around six, Sean disappeared. Lorne saw him reappear and stand at the end of the table. Someone switched the music off, and everyone's attention turned his way.

"Lorne, if you'd care to join me."

Tony kissed her on the forehead when she glanced up at him, puzzled. "Go."

She was feeling a little tipsy. She'd only had a couple of glasses of wine what with her still being on the course of painkillers. "Sean? What's this all about?"

He reached behind him and picked up some form of trophy from the table. "It is with the greatest of honour, I present to you a long service award from the Met. The police force will never be the same without you, Lorne Simpkins/Warner."

Her mouth gaped open, and she struggled to hold back the dam which had burst. Finally finding her voice, she said, "Oh gosh, I never expected this. Tony, I hope you've saved some of that bubble wrap for this beauty?"

The crowd laughed.

"It's all in hand, don't worry," he shouted back, his expression full of pride.

"Thank you. None of this would have been possible without the best team around by my side. Take a bow, the lot of you. I'm going to miss you all; however, I'm passing over the baton to someone more than capable of filling my shoes." She held out a hand for Katy to take.

They shared a hug.

Charlie joined them for a group hug, her own tears flowing freely. "Mum, we have one more surprise for you."

Lorne frowned and waited for her daughter to continue.

Sean moved position and stood between Katy and Charlie, an arm around each of their shoulders. "Welcome to the new A-Team. Katy will be filling your shoes, and Charlie has agreed to join the team and work alongside her."

"What? Why didn't someone tell me?" She shot a glance in Tony's direction.

He was laughing and raised his glass.

"It was only a matter of time before another Simpkins joined the team," he shouted.

As much as she tried to stem the flow of tears, she found it impossible. Pulling Charlie into her arms, she whispered, "I'm so damn proud of you, young lady. You've come a long way in such a short time."

"Enjoy your retirement, Mum. We all love you and wish you the best with the challenges that lie ahead of you."

Tony and Brandon joined them for another group hug.

Lorne's heart was ready to explode; she was surrounded by people who loved her. She truly was the luckiest woman alive.

THE END

NOTE TO THE READER

Dear reader,

I hope you enjoyed the final ever Justice book, it's time for Lorne and the team to go their separate ways, but watch out for a spin-off series starring Katy and Charlie early 2020.

If you enjoy my work, perhaps you'll consider reading some of the other series I have penned over the past few years. I'm sure you'll enjoy the Ellie Brazil PI series. The first book is SOLE INTENTION

As always, thank you for choosing to read my book out of the millions available today. If you could find it in your heart to leave a review, I'd truly appreciate it, I read every single one of them.

M. A. Comley